CHAPTER I

Halfway up the shining surface of the gilt-framed pier glass was a mark—a tiny ink-line that had been carefully drawn across the outer edge of the wide bevel. As Gwendolyn stared at the line, the reflection of her small face in the mirror grew suddenly all white, as if some rude hand had reached out and brushed away the pink from cheeks and lips. Arms rigid at her sides, and open palms pressed hard against the flaring skirts of her riding-coat, she shrank back from the glass.

"Oo-oo!" she breathed, aghast. The gray eyes swam.

After a moment, however, she blinked resolutely to clear her sight, stepped forward again, and, straightening her slender little figure to its utmost height, measured herself a second time against the mirror.

But—as before—the top of her yellow head did not reach above the ink-mark—not by the smallest part of an inch! So there was no longer any reason to hope! The worst was true! She had drawn the tiny line across the edge of the bevel the evening before, when she was only six years old; now it was mid-morning of another day, and she was seven—*yet she was not a whit taller!*

The tears began to overflow. She pressed her embroidered handkerchief to her eyes. Then, stifling a sob, she crossed the nursery, stumbling once or twice as she made toward the long cushioned seat that stretched the whole width of the front window. There, among the down-filled pillows, with her loose hair falling about her wet cheeks and screening them, she lay down.

For months she had looked forward with secret longing to this seventh anniversary. Every morning she had taken down the rose-embossed calendar that stood on the top of her gold-and-white writing-desk and tallied off another of the days that intervened before her birthday. And the previous evening she had measured herself against the pier glass without even a single misgiving.

She rose at an early hour. Her waking look was toward the pier glass. Her one thought was to gauge her new height. But the morning was the usual busy one. When Jane finished bathing and dressing her, Miss Royle summoned her to breakfast. An hour in the school-room followed—an hour of quiet study, but under the watchful eye of the governess. Next, Gwendolyn changed her dressing-gown for a riding-habit, and with Jane holding her by one small hand, and with Thomas following, stepped into the bronze cage that dropped down so noiselessly from nursery floor to wide entrance-hall. Outside, the limousine was waiting. She and Jane entered it. Thomas took his seat beside the chauffeur. And in a moment the motor was speeding away.

At the riding-school, her master gave her the customary lesson: She circled the tanbark on her fat brown pony—now to the right, at a walk; now to the left, at a trot; now back to the right again at a rattling canter, with her yellow hair whipping her shoulders, and her three-cornered hat working farther and farther back on her bobbing head, and tugging hard at the elastic under her dimpled chin. After nearly an hour of this walk, trot and canter she was very rosy, and quite out of breath. Then she was put back into the limousine and driven swiftly home. And it was not until after her arrival that she had a moment entirely to herself, and the first opportunity of comparing her height with the tiny ink-line on the edge of the mirror's bevel.

Now as she lay, face down, on the window-seat, she know how vain had been all the longing of months. The realization, so sudden and unexpected, was a blow. The slender little figure among the cushions quivered under it.

But all at once she sat up. And disappointment and grief gave place to apprehension. "I wonder what's the matter with me," she faltered aloud. "Oh, something awful, I guess."

The next moment caution succeeded fear. She sprang to her feet and ran across the room. That tell-tale mark was still on the mirror, for nurse or governess to see and question. And it was advisable that no one should learn the unhappy truth. Her handkerchief was damp with tears. She gathered the tiny square of linen into a tight ball and rubbed at the ink-line industriously.

She was not a moment too soon. Scarcely had she regained the window-seat, when the hall door opened and Thomas appeared on the sill, almost filling the opening with his tall figure. As a rule he wore his very splendid footman's livery of dark blue coat with dull-gold buttons, blue trousers, and striped buff waistcoat. Now he wore street clothes, and he had a leash in his hand.

"Is Jane about, Miss Gwendolyn?" he inquired. Then, seeing that Gwendolyn was alone, "Would you mind tellin' her when she comes that I'm out takin' the Madam's dogs for a walk?"

Gwendolyn had a new thought. "A—a walk?" she repeated. And stood up.

"But tell Jane, if you please," continued he, "that I'll be back in time to go— well, *she* knows where." This was said significantly. He turned.

"Thomas!" Gwendolyn hastened across to him. "Wait till I put on my hat. I'm—I'm going with you." Her riding-hat lay among the dainty pink-and-white articles on her crystal-topped dressing-table. She caught it up.

"Miss Gwendolyn!" exclaimed Thomas, astonished.

"I'm seven," declared Gwendolyn, struggling with the hat-elastic. "I'm a whole year older than I was yesterday. And—and I'm grown-up."

An exasperating smile lifted Thomas's lip. "Oh, *are* you!" he observed.

The hat settled, she met his look squarely. (Did he suspicion anything?) "*Yes*. And you take the dogs out to walk. So"—she started to pass him —"*I'm* going to walk."

His hair was black and straight. Now it seemed fairly to bristle with amazement. "I couldn't take you if you *was* grown-up," he asserted firmly, blocking her advance; "—leastways not without Miss Royle or Jane'd say Yes. It'd be worth my job."

Gwendolyn lowered her eyes, stood a moment in indecision, then pulled off the hat, tossed it aside, went back to the window, and sat down.

At one end of the seat, swung high on its gilded spring, danced the dome-topped cage of her canary. Presently she raised her face to him. He was traveling tirelessly from perch to cage-floor, from floor to trapeze again. His wings were half lifted from his little body—the bright yellow of her own hair. It was as if he were ready for flight. His round black eyes were constantly turned toward the world beyond the window. He perked his head inquiringly, and cheeped. Now and then, with a wild beating of his pinions, he sprang sidewise to the shining bars of the cage, and hung there, panting.

She watched him for a time; made a slow survey of the nursery next,—and sighed.

"Poor thing!" she murmured.

She heard the rustle of silk skirts from the direction of the school-room. Hastily she shook out the embroidered handkerchief and put it against her eyes.

A door opened. "There will be no lessons this afternoon, Gwendolyn." It was Miss Royle's voice.

Gwendolyn did not speak. But she lowered the handkerchief a trifle—and noted that the governess was dressed for going out—in a glistening black silk plentifully ornamented with jet *paillettes*.

Miss Royle rustled her way to the pier-glass to have a last look at her bonnet. It was a poke, with a quilted ribbon circling its brim, and some lace arranged fluffily. It did not reach many inches above the spot where Gwendolyn had drawn the ink-line, for Miss Royle was small. When she had given the poke a pat here and a touch there, she leaned forward to get a better view of her face. She had a pale, thin face and thin faded hair. On either side of a high bony nose were set her pale-blue eyes. Shutting them in, and perched on the thinnest part of her nose, were silver-circled spectacles.

"I'm very glad I can give you a half-holiday, dear," she went on. But her tone was somewhat sorrowful. She detached a small leaf of paper from a tiny book in her hand-bag and rubbed it across her forehead. "For my neuralgia is *much* worse to-day." She coughed once or twice behind a lisle-gloved hand, snapped the clasp of her hand-bag and started toward the hall door.

It was now that for the first time she looked at Gwendolyn—and caught sight of the bowed head, the grief-flushed cheeks, the suspended handkerchief. She stopped short.

"Gwendolyn!" she exclaimed, annoyed. "I *hope* you're not going to be cross and troublesome, and make it impossible for me to have a couple of hours to myself this afternoon—especially when I'm suffering." Then, coaxingly, "You can amuse yourself with one of your nice pretend-games, dear."

From under long up-curling lashes Gwendolyn regarded her in silence.

"I've planned to lunch out," went on Miss Royle. "But you won't mind, *will* you, dear Gwendolyn?" plaintively. "For I'll be back at tea-time. And besides"—growing brighter—"you're to have—what do you think!—the birthday cake Cook has made."

"I *hate* cake!" burst out Gwendolyn; and covered her eyes once more.

"*Gwen-do-lyn!*" breathed Miss Royle.

Gwendolyn sat very still.

"How *can* you be so naughty! Oh, it's really wicked and ungrateful of you to be fretting and complaining—you who have *so* many blessings! But you don't appreciate them because you've always had them. Well,"—mournfully solicitous—"I trust they'll never be taken from you, my child. Ah, *I* know how bitter such a loss is! I haven't *always* been in my present circumstances, compelled to go out among strangers to earn a scant living. Once—"

Here she was interrupted. The door from the school-room swung wide with a bang. Gwendolyn, looking up, saw her nurse.

Jane was in sharp contrast to Miss Royle—taller and stocky, with broad shoulders and big arms. As she halted against the open school-room door, her hair was as ruddy as the panel that made a background for it. And she had reddish eyes, and a full round face. In the midst of her face, and all out of proportion to it, was her short turned-up nose, which was plentifully sprinkled with freckles.

"So you're goin' out?" she began angrily, addressing the governess.

Miss Royle retreated a step. "Just for a—a couple of hours," she explained.

Jane's face grew almost as red as her hair. Slamming the school-room door behind her, she advanced. "I suppose it's the neuralgia again," she suggested with quiet heat.

The color stole into Miss Royle's pale cheeks. She coughed. "It *is* a little worse than usual this afternoon," she admitted.

"I thought so," said Jane. "It's always worse—*on bargain-days*."

"How *dare* you!"

"You ask me that, do you?—you old snake-in-the-grass!" Now Jane grew pallid with anger.

Gwendolyn, listening, contemplated her governess thoughtfully. She had often heard her pronounced a snake-in-the-grass.

Miss Royle was also pale. "That will do!" she declared. "I shall report you to Madam."

"Report!" echoed Jane, giving a loud, harsh laugh, and shaking her hair—the huge pompadour in front, the pug behind. "Well, go ahead. And I'll report *you*—and your handy neuralgia."

"It's your duty to look after Gwendolyn when there are no lessons," reminded Miss Royle, but weakening noticeably.

"On *week*-days?" shrilled Jane. "Oh, don't try to fool me with any of your schemin'! *I* see. And I just laugh in my sleeve!"

Gwendolyn fixed inquiring gray eyes upon that sleeve of Jane's dress which was the nearer. It was of black sateen. It fitted the stout arm sleekly.

"This is the dear child's birthday, and I wish her to have the afternoon free."

"A-a-ah! Then why don't you take her out with you? You like the auto*mo*bile nice enough,"—this sneeringly.

Miss Royle tossed her head. "I thought perhaps *you'd* be using the car," she answered, with fine sarcasm.

Jane began to argue, throwing out both hands: "How was *I* to know to-day was her birthday? You might've told me about it; instead, just all of a sudden, you shove her off on my hands."

Gwendolyn's eyes narrowed resentfully.

Miss Royle gave a quick look toward the window-seat. "You mean you've made plans?" she asked, concern supplanting anger in her voice.

To all appearances Jane was near to tears. She did not answer. She nodded dejectedly.

"Well, Jane, you shall have to-morrow afternoon," declared Miss Royle, soothingly. "Is *that* fair? I didn't know you'd counted on to-day. So—" Here another glance shot window-ward. Then she beckoned Jane. They went into the hall. And Gwendolyn heard them whispering together.

When Jane came back into the nursery she looked almost cheerful. "Now off with that habit," she called to Gwendolyn briskly. "And into something for your dinner."

"I want to wear a plaid dress," announced Gwendolyn, getting down from her seat slowly.

Jane was selecting a white muslin from a tall wardrobe. "Little girls ain't wearin' plaids this year," she declared shortly. "Come."

"Well, then, I want a dress that's got a pocket," went on Gwendolyn, "—a pocket 'way down on this side." She touched the right skirt of her riding-coat.

"They ain't makin' pockets in little girls' dresses this year," said Jane, "Come! Come!"

"'They,'" repeated Gwendolyn. "Who are 'They'? I'd like to know; 'cause I could telephone 'em and—"

"Hush your nonsense!" bade Jane. Then, catching at the delicate square of linen in Gwendolyn's hand, "How'd you git ink smeared over your handkerchief? What do you suppose your mamma'd say if she was to come upon it? *I'd* be blamed—*as* usual!"

"Who are They'?" persisted Gwendolyn. "'They' do so *many* things. And I want to tell 'em that I like pockets in *all* my dresses."

Jane ignored the question.

"Yesterday you said 'They' would send us soda-water," went on Gwendolyn —talking to herself now, rather than to the nurse. "And I'd like to know where 'They' *find* soda-water." Whereupon she fell to pondering the question. Evidently this, like many another propounded to Jane or Miss Royle; to Thomas; to her music-teacher, Miss Brown; to Mademoiselle Du Bois, her French teacher; and to her teacher of German, was one that was meant to remain a secret of the grown-ups.

Jane, having unbuttoned the riding-coat, pulled at the small black boots. She was also talking to herself, for her lips moved.

The moment Gwendolyn caught sight of her unshod feet, she had a new idea—the securing of a long-denied privilege by urging the occasion. "Oh, Jane," she cried. "May I go barefoot?—just for a *little* while. I want to." Jane stripped off the cobwebby stockings. Gwendolyn wriggled her ten pink toes. "May I, Jane?"

"You can go barefoot to *bed*," said Jane.

Gwendolyn's bed stood midway of the nursery, partly hidden by a high tapestried screen. It was a beautiful bed, carved and enamelled, and panelled—head and foot—with woven cane. But to Gwendolyn it was, by day, a white instrument of torture. She gave it a glance of disfavor now, and refrained from pursuing her idea.

When the muslin dress was donned, and a pink satin hair-bow replaced the black one that bobbed on Gwendolyn's head when she rode, she returned to the window and sat down. The seat was deep, and her shiny patent-leather slippers stuck straight out in front of her. In one hand she held a fresh handkerchief. She nibbled at it thoughtfully. She was still wondering about "They."

Thomas looked cross when he came in to serve her noon dinner. He arranged the table with a jerk and a bang.

"So old Royle up and outed, did she?" he said to Jane.

"Hush!" counseled Jane, significantly, and rolled her eyes in the direction of the window-seat.

Gwendolyn stopped nibbling her handkerchief.

"And our plans is spoiled," went on Thomas. "Well, ain't that our luck! And I suppose you couldn't manage to leave a certain party—"

Gwendolyn had been watching Thomas. Now she fell to observing the silver buckles on her slippers. She might not know who "They" were. But "a certain party"—

"Leave?" repeated Jane, "Who with? Not alone, surely you don't mean. For something's gone wrong already to-day, as you'll see if you'll use your eyes. And a fuss or a howl'd mean that somebody'd hear, and tattle to the Madam, and—"

Thomas said something under his breath.

"So we can't go after all," resumed Jane; "—leastways not like we'd counted on. And it's *too* exasperatin'. Here I am, a person that likes my freedom once in a while, and a glimpse at the shop-windows,—exactly as much as old you-know-who does—and a bit of tea afterwards with a—a friend."

At this point, Gwendolyn glanced up—just in time to see Thomas regarding Jane with a broad grin. And Jane was smiling back at him, her face so suffused with blushes that there was not a freckle to be seen.

Now Jane sighed, and stood looking down with hands folded. "What good does it do to talk, though," she observed sadly. "Day in and day out, day *in* and day out, I have to dance attendance."

It was Gwendolyn's turn to color. She got down quickly and came forward.

"Sh!" warned Thomas. He busied himself with laying the silver.

Gwendolyn halted in front of Jane, and lifted a puzzled face. "But—but, Jane," she began defensively, "you don't ever *dance*."

"Now, whatever do you think I was talkin' about?" demanded Jane, roughly. "You dance, don't you, at Monsoor Tellegen's, of a Saturday afternoon? Well, so do I when I get a' evenin' off,—which isn't often, as you well know, Miss. And now your dinner's ready. So eat it, without any more clackin'."

Gwendolyn climbed upon the plump rounding seat of a white-and-gold chair.

Jane settled down nearby, choosing an upholstered arm-chair—spacious, comfort-giving. She lolled in it, at ease but watchful.

"You can't think how that old butler spies on me," said Thomas, addressing her. "He seen the tray when I put it on the dumb-waiter. And, 'Miss Royle is havin' her lunch out,' he says. Then would you *believe* it, he took more'n half my dishes away!"

Jane giggled. "Potter's a sharp one," she declared. "But, oh, you should've been behind a door just now when you-know-who and I had a little understandin'."

"Eh?" he inquired, working his black brows excitedly. "How was that?"

Gwendolyn went calmly on with her mutton-broth. She already knew each detail of the forth-coming recital.

"Well," began Jane, "she played her usual trick of startin' off without so much as a word to me, and I just up and give her a tongue-lashin'."

Gwendolyn's spoon paused half way to her expectant pink mouth. She stared at Jane. "Oh, I didn't see that," she exclaimed regretfully. "Jane, what is a tongue-lashing?"

Jane sat up. "A tongue-lashin'," said she, "is what *you* need, young lady. Look at the way you've spilled your soup! Take it, Thomas, and serve the rest of the dinner, I ain't goin' to allow you to be at the table *all* day, Miss.... There, Thomas! That'll be all the minced chicken she can have."

"But I took just one little spoonful," protested Gwendolyn, earnestly. "I wanted more, but Thomas held it 'way up, and—"

"Do you want to be sick?" demanded Jane. "And have a doctor come?"

Gwendolyn raised frightened eyes. A doctor had been called once in the dim past, when she was a baby, racked by colic and budding teeth. She did not remember him. But since the era of short clothes she had been mercifully spared his visits. "N-n-no!" she faltered.

"Well, you look out or I'll git one on the 'phone. And you'll be sorry *the rest of your life*.... Take the chicken away, Thomas. 'Out of sight is'—you know the sayin'. (It's a pity there ain't some way to keep it hot.)"

"A bit of cold fowl don't go so bad," said Thomas, reassuringly. And to Gwendolyn, "Here's more of the potatoes souffles, Miss Gwendolyn,—*very* tasty and fillin'."

Gwendolyn put up a hand and pushed the proffered dish aside.

"Now, no temper," warned Jane, rising. "Too much meat ain't good for children. Your mamma herself would say that. Come! See that nice potatoes and cream gravy on your plate. And there you set cryin'!"

Thomas had an idea. "Shall I fetch the cake?" he asked in a loud whisper.

Jane nodded.

He disappeared—to reappear at once with a round frosted cake that had a border of pink icing upon its glazed white top. And set within the circle of the border were seven pink candles, all alight.

"Oh, look! Look!" cried Jane, excitedly, pulling Gwendolyn's hand away from her eyes. "Isn't it a beautiful cake! You shall have a bi-i-ig piece."

Those seven small candles dispelled the gloom. With tears on her cheeks, but all eager and smiling once more, Gwendolyn blew the candles out. And as she bent forward to puff at each tiny one, Jane held her bright hair back, for fear that a strand might get too near a flame.

"Oh, Jane," cried Gwendolyn, "when I blow like that, *where* do all the little lights go?"

"Did you ever *hear* such a question?" exclaimed Jane, appealing to Thomas.

He was cutting away at the cake. "Of course, Miss, you'd like *me* to have a bite of this," he said. "You know it was me that reminded Cook about bakin'—"

"Perhaps all the little lights go up under the big lamp-shade," went on Gwendolyn, too absorbed to listen to Thomas. "And make a big light." She started to get down from her chair to investigate.

"Now look here," said Jane irritably, "you'll just finish your dinner before you leave the table. Here's your cake. *Eat* it!"

Gwendolyn ate her slice daintily, using a fork.

Jane also ate a slice—holding it in her fingers. "There's ways of managin' a fairly jolly afternoon," she said from the depths of the arm-chair.

"You're speakin' of—er—?" asked Thomas, picking up cake crumbs with a damp finger-tip.

"Uh-huh."

"A certain party would have to go along," he reminded.

"*Of* course. But a ride's better'n nothin'."

"Shall I telephone for—?" Thomas brought a finger-bowl.

Gwendolyn stood up. A ride meant the limousine, with its screening top and little windows. The limousine meant a long, tiresome run at good speed through streets that she longed to travel afoot, slowly, with a stop here and a stop there, and a poke into things in general.

Her crimson cheeks spoke rebellion. "I want a walk this afternoon," she declared emphatically.

"Use your finger-bowl," said Jane. "Can't you *never* remember your manners?"

"I'm seven today," Gwendolyn went on, the tips of her fingers in the small basin of silver while her face was turned to Jane. "I'm seven and—and I'm grown-up."

"And you're splashin' water on the table-cloth. Look at you!"

"So," went on Gwendolyn, "I'm going to walk. I haven't walked for a whole, whole week."

"You can lean back in the car," began Jane enthusiastically, "and pretend you're a grand little Queen!"

"I don't *want* to be a Queen. I want to *walk.*

"Rich little girls don't hike along the streets like common poor little girls," informed Jane.

"I don't *want* to be a rich little girl,"—voice shrill with determination.

Jane went to shake her frilled apron into the gilded waste-basket beside Gwendolyn's writing-desk. "You can telephone any time now, Thomas," she said calmly.

Gwendolyn turned upon Thomas. "But I don't *want* to be shut up in the car this afternoon," she cried. "And I won't! I *won't!* I WON'T!"

Jane gave a gasp of smothered rage. The reddish eyes blazed. "Do you want me to send for a great black bear?" she demanded.

At that Gwendolyn quailed. "No-o-o!"

Jane shot a glance toward Thomas. It invited suggestion.

"Let her take something along," he said under his breath, nodding toward a glass-fronted case of shelves that stood opposite Gwendolyn's bed.

Each shelf of the case was covered with toys. Along one sat a line of daintily clad dolls—black-haired dolls; golden-haired dolls; dolls from China, with slanted eyes and a queue; dolls from Japan, in gayly figured kimonos; Dutch dolls—a boy and a girl; a French doll in an exquisite frock; a Russian; an Indian; a Spaniard. A second shelf held a shiny red-and-black peg-top, a black wooden snake beside its lead-colored pipe-like case; a tin soldier in an English uniform—red coat, and pill-box cap held on by a chin-strap; a second uniformed tin man who turned somersaults, but in repose stood upon his head; a black dog on wheels, with great floppy ears; and a half-dozen downy ducklings acquired at Easter.

"Much good takin' anything'll do!" grumbled Jane. Then, plucking crossly at a muslin sleeve, "Well, what do you want? Your French doll? Speak up!"

"I don't want anything," asserted Gwendolyn, "—long as I can't have my Puffy Bear any more." There was a wide vacant place beside the dog with the large ears.

"The little beast got shabby," explained Thomas, "and I was compelled to throw him away along with the old linen-hamper. Like as not some poor little child has him now."

She considered the statement, gray eyes wistful. Then, "I liked him," she said huskily. "He was old and squashy, and it wouldn't hurt him to walk up the Drive, right in the path where the horses go. The dirt is loose there, like it was in the road at Johnnie Blake's in the country. I could scuff it with my shoes."

"You could scuff it and I could wear myself out cleanin', I suppose," retorted Jane. "And like as not run the risk of gittin' some bad germs on my hands, and dyin' of 'em. From what Rosa says, it was downright *shameful* the way you muddied your clothes, and tore 'em, and messed in the water after nasty tad-poles that week you was up country. *I* won't allow you to treat your beautiful dresses like that, or climb about, or let the hot sun git at you."

"I'm going to *walk*."

Silence; but silence palpitant with thought. Then Jane threw up her head— as if seized with an inspiration. "You're going to walk?" said she. "All right! *All* right! Walk if you want to." She made as if to set out. "*Go* ahead! But, my *dear*," (she dropped her voice in fear) "you'll no more'n git to the next corner when *somebody'll steal you!*"

Gwendolyn was silent for a long moment. She glanced from Jane to Thomas, from Thomas to Jane, and crooked her fingers in and out of her twisted handkerchief.

"But, Jane," she said finally, "the dogs go out walking—and—and nobody steals the dogs."

"Hear the silly child!" cried Jane. "Nobody steals the dogs! Why, if anybody was to steal the dogs what good would it do 'em? They're only Pomeranians anyhow, and Madam could go straight out and buy more. Besides, like as not Pomeranians won't be stylish next year, and so Madam wouldn't care two snaps. She'd go buy the latest thing in poodles, or else a fine collie, or a spaniel or a Spitz."

"But other little girls walk all the time," insisted Gwendolyn, "and nobody steals *them*."

Jane crossed her knees, pursed her mouth and folded her arms. "Well, Thomas," she said, shaking her head, "I guess after all that I'll have to tell her."

"Ah, yes, I suppose so," agreed Thomas. His tone was funereal.

Gwendolyn looked from one to the other.

"I haven't wanted to," continued Jane, dolefully. "*You* know that. But now she forces me to do it. Though I'm as sorry as sorry can be."

Thomas had just taken his portion of cake in one great mouthful. "Fo'm my," he chimed in.

Gwendolyn looked concerned. "But I'm seven," she reiterated.

"Seven?" said Jane. "What has that got to do with it? *Age* don't matter."

Gwendolyn did not flinch.

"You said nobody steals other little girls," went on Jane. "It ain't true. Poor little girls and boys, *no*body steals. You can see 'em runnin' around loose everywheres. But it's different when a little girl's papa is made of money."

"So much money," added Thomas, "that it fairly makes me palm itch." Whereat he fell to rubbing one open hand against a corner of the piano.

Gwendolyn reflected a moment. Then, "But my fath-er isn't made of money,"—she lingered a little, tenderly, over the word father, pronouncing it as if it were two words. "I *know* he isn't. When I was at Johnnie Blake's cottage, we went fishing, and fath-er rolled up his sleeves. And his arms were strong; and red, like Jane's."

Thomas sniggered.

But Jane gestured impatiently. Then, making scared eyes, "What has that *got to do*," she demanded, "*with the wicked men that keep watch of this house?*"

Gwendolyn swallowed. "What wicked men?" she questioned apprehensively.

"Ah-ha!" triumphed Jane. "I *thought* that'd catch you! Now just let me ask you another question: *Why are there bars on the basement windows?*"

Gwendolyn's lips parted to reply. But no words came.

"You don't know," said Jane. "But I'll tell you something: There ain't no bars on the windows where *poor* little girls live. For the simple reason that nobody wants to steal *them*."

Gwendolyn considered the statement, her fingers still busy knotting and unknotting.

"I tell you," Jane launched forth again, "that if you run about on the street, like poor children do, you'll be grabbed up by a band of kidnapers."

"Are—are kidnapers worse than doctors?" asked Gwendolyn.

"Worse than doctors!" scoffed Thomas, "*Heaps* worse."

"Worse than—than bears?" (The last trace of that rebellious red was gone.)

Up and down went Jane's head solemnly. "Kidnapers carry knives—big curved knives."

Now Gwendolyn recalled a certain terror-inspiring man with a long belted coat and a cap with a shiny visor. It was not his height that made her fear him, for her father was fully as tall; and it was not his brass-buttoned coat, or the dark, piercing eyes under the visor. She feared him because Jane had often threatened her with his coming; and, secondly, because he wore, hanging from his belt, a cudgel—long and heavy and thick. How that cudgel glistened in the sunlight as it swung to and fro by a thong!

"Worse than a—a p'liceman?" she faltered.

"Policeman? *Yes!*"

"Than the p'liceman that's—that's always hanging around here?"

Now Jane giggled, and blushed as red as her hair. "Hush!" she chided.

Thomas poked a teasing finger at her. "Haw! Haw!" he laughed. "There's other people that's noticed a policeman hangin' round. *He's* a dandy, he is! —*not.* He let that old hand organ man give him a black eye."

"Pooh!" retorted Jane. "You know how much I care about that policeman! It's only that I like to have him handy for just such times as this."

But Gwendolyn was dwelling on the newly discovered scourge of moneyed children. "What would the kidnapers do?" she inquired.

"The kidnapers," promptly answered Jane, "would take you and shut you up in a nasty cellar, where there was rats and mice and things and—"

Gwendolyn's mouth began to quiver.

Hastily Jane put out a hand. "But we'll look sharp that nothin' of the kind happens," she declared stoutly; "for who can git you when you're in the car —*especially* when Thomas is along to watch out. So"—with a great show of enthusiasm—"we'll go out, oh! for a *grand* ride." She rose. "And maybe when we git into the country a ways, we'll invite Thomas to take the inside seat opposite," (another wink) "and he'll tell you about soldierin' in India, and camps, and marches, and shootin' elephants."

"Aren't there kidnapers in the country, too?" asked Gwendolyn. "I—I guess I'd rather stay home."

"You won't see 'em in the country this time of day," explained Jane. "They're all in town, huntin' rich little children. So on with the sweet new hat and a pretty coat!" She opened the door of the wardrobe.

Gwendolyn did not move. But as she watched Jane the gray eyes filled with tears, which overflowed and trickled slowly down her cheeks. "If—if Thomas walked along with us," she began, "could—could anybody steal me then?"

Jane was taking out coat, hat and gloves. "What would kidnapers care about *Thomas?*" she demanded contemptuously. "*Sure*, they'd steal you, and then they'd say to your father, 'Give! me a million dollars in cash if you want Miss Gwendolyn back.' And if your father didn't give the money on the spot, you'd be sold to gipsies, or—or *Chinamen.*"

But Gwendolyn persisted. "Thomas has killed el'phunts," she reminded. "Are—are kidnapers worse than el'phunts?" She drew on her gloves.

Jane sat down and held out the coat. It was of velvet. "Now be still!" she commanded roughly. "You'll go in the machine if you go at *all*. Do you hear that?"—giving Gwendolyn a half-turn-about that nearly upset her. "Do you think I'm goin' to trapse over the hard pavements on my poor, tired feet just because *you* take your notions?"

Gwendolyn began to cry—softly. "Oh, I—I thought I wouldn't ever have to ride again wh-when I was seven," she faltered, putting one white-gloved hand to her eyes.

"Stop that!" commanded Jane, again, "Dirtyin' your gloves, you wasteful little thing!"

Now the big sobs came. Down went the yellow head.

"Oh! Oh! Oh!" said Thomas. "Little *ladies* never cry."

"Walk! walk! walk!" scolded Jane, kneeling, and preparing to adjust the new hat.

The hat had wide ribbons that tied under the chin—new, stiff ribbons.

"Johnnie Bu-Blake didn't fasten *his* hat on like this," wept Gwendolyn. She moved her chin from side to side. "He just had a—a sh-shoe-string."

Jane had finished. "Johnnie Blake! Johnnie Blake! Johnnie Blake!" she mocked. She gave Gwendolyn a little push toward the front window. "Now, no more of your nonsense. Go and be quiet for a few minutes. And keep a' eye out, will you, to see that there's nobody layin' in wait for us out in front?"

Gwendolyn went forward to the window-seat and climbed up among its cushions. From there she looked down upon the Drive with its sloping, evenly-cut grass, its smooth, tawny road and soft brown bridle-path, and its curving walk, stone-walled on the outer side. Beyond park and road and walk were tree-tops, bush-high above the wall. And beyond these was the broad, slow-flowing river, with boats going to and fro upon its shimmering surface. The farther side of the river was walled like the walk, only the wall was a cliff, sheer and dark and timber-edged. And through this timber could be seen the roofs and chimneys of distant houses.

But Gwendolyn saw nothing of the beauty of the view. She did not even glance down to where, on its pedestal, stood the great bronze war-horse, its mane and tail flying, its neck arched, its lips curved to neigh. Astride the horse was her friend, the General, soldierly, valorous, his hat doffed—as if in silent greeting to the double procession of vehicles and pedestrians that was passing before him. Brave he might be, but what help was the General *now?*

When Jane was ready for the drive, Gwendolyn took a firm hold of one thick thumb. And, with Thomas following, they were soon in the entrance hall. There, waiting as usual, was Potter, the butler. He smiled at Gwendolyn.

But Gwendolyn did not smile in return. As the cage had sunk swiftly down the long shaft, her heart had sunk, too. And now she thought how old Potter was; how thin and stooped. With kidnapers about, was *he* a fit guardian for the front door? As Potter swung wide the heavy grille of wrought iron, with its silk-hung back of plate-glass, Gwendolyn pulled hard at Jane's hand, and went down the granite steps and across the sidewalk as quickly as possible, with a timid glance to right and left. For, even as she entered the car, might not that band of knife-men suddenly catch sight of her, and, rushing over walk and bridle-path and roadway, seize her and carry her off?

She sank, trembling, upon the seat of the limousine.

Jane followed her. Then Thomas closed the windowed door of the motor and took his place beside the chauffeur.

Gwendolyn leaned forward for a swift glance at the lower windows, barred against intruders. The great house was of stone. On side and rear it stood flat against other houses. But it was built on a corner; and along its front and outer side, the tops of the basement windows were set a foot or more above the level of the sidewalk. To Gwendolyn those windows were huge eyes, peering out at her from under heavy lashes of iron.

The automobile started. Jane arranged her skirts and leaned back luxuriously, her big hands folded on her lap.

"My! but ain't this grand!" she exclaimed. Then to Gwendolyn: "You don't mind, do you, dearie, if Jane has a taste of gum as we go along?"

Gwendolyn did not reply. She had not heard. She was leaning toward the little window on her side of the limousine. In front of Jane was the chauffeur, wide-backed and skillful, and crouched vigilantly over his wheel. But in front of her was Thomas, sitting in the proudly erect, stiff position peculiar to him whenever he fared abroad. He looked neither to right nor left. He seemed indifferent that danger lurked for her along the Drive.

But she—! As the limousine joined others, all speeding forward merrily, her pale little face was pressed against the shield-shaped pane of glass, her frightened eyes roved continually, searching the moving crowds.

CHAPTER II

The nursery was on the top-most floor of the great stone house—this for sunshine and air. But the sunshine was gone when Gwendolyn returned from her drive, and a half-dozen silk-shaded lights threw a soft glow over the room. To shut out the chill of the spring evening the windows were down. Across them were drawn the heavy hangings of rose brocade.

There was a lamp on the larger of the nursery tables, a tall lamp, almost flower-like with its petal-shaped ruffles of lace and chiffon. It made conspicuous two packages that flanked it—one small and square; the other large, and as round as a hat-box. Each was wrapped in white paper and tied with red string.

"Birthday presents!" cried Jane, the moment she spied them; and sprang forward. "Oh, I wonder what they are! What do *you* guess, Gwendolyn?"

Gwendolyn followed slowly, blinking against the light. "I can't guess," she said without enthusiasm. The glass-fronted case was full of toys, none of which she particularly cherished. (Indeed, most of them were carefully wrapped from sight.) New ones would merely form an addition.

"Well, what would you *like?*" queried Jane, catching up the small package and shaking it.

Gwendolyn suddenly looked very earnest.

"Most in the whole *world?*" she asked.

"Yes, what?" Jane dropped the small package and shook the large one.

"In the whole, whole big world?" went on Gwendolyn—to herself rather than to her nurse. She was not looking at the table, but toward a curtained window, and the gray eyes had a tender faraway expression. There was a faint conventional pattern in the brocade of the heavy hangings. It suggested trees with graceful down-growing boughs. She clasped her hands.

"I want to live out in the woods," she said, "at Johnnie Blake's cottage by the stream that's got fish in it."

Jane set the big package down with a thump. "That's *awful* selfish of you," she declared warmly. "For you know right well that Thomas and *I* wouldn't like to leave the city and live away out in the country. *Would* we, Thomas?"—for he had just entered.

"Cer-tain-ly *not*," said Thomas.

"And it'd give poor Miss Royle the neuralgia," (Jane and Miss Royle might contend with each other; they made common cause against *her*.)

"But none of you'd *have* to" assured Gwendolyn. "When I was at Johnnie Blake's that once, just Potter went, and Rosa, and Cook. And Rosa buttoned my dresses and gave me my bath, and—"

"So Rosa'll do *just* as well as me," interrupted Jane, jealously.

"—And Potter passed the dishes at table," resumed Gwendolyn, ignoring the remark; "and *he* never hurried the best-tasting ones."

"Hear that will you, Thomas!" cried Jane. "Mr. *Potter* never hurried the best-tastin' ones!"

Thomas gave her a significant stare. "I tell you, a certain person is growin' keen," he said in a low voice.

Jane took Gwendolyn by the arm. "Put all that Johnnie Blake nonsense out of your head," she commanded. "Folks that live in the woods don't know nothin'. They're silly and pokey."

Gwendolyn shook her head with deliberation. "Johnny Blake wasn't pokey," she denied. "He had a willow fishpole, and a string tied to it. And he caught shiny fishes on the end of the string."

"Johnnie Blake!" sniffed Jane. "Oh, I know all about *him*. Rosa told me. He's a common, poor little boy. And"—severely—"I, for *one*, can't see why you was ever allowed to play with him!...

"Now, darlin',"—softening—"here we stand fussin', and you ain't even guessed what your presents are. Guess something that's real fine: something you'd like in the city, pettie." She began to unwrap the larger of the packages.

"Oh," said Gwendolyn. "What I'd like in the *city*. Well,"—suddenly between her brows there came a curious, strained little wrinkle—"I'd like —"

The white paper fell away. A large, round box was disclosed. To it was tied a small card.

"This is from your papa!" cried Jane. "Oh, let's see what it is!"

The wrinkle smoothed. A smile broke,—like sudden sunlight after clouds, and shadow. Then there poured forth all that had filled her heart during the past months:

"I'd like to eat at the grown-up table with my fath-er and my moth-er," she declared; "and I don't want to have a nurse any more like a baby! and I want to go to *day*-school."

Jane gasped, and her big hands fell from the round box. Thomas stared, and reddened even to his ears, which were large and over-prominent. To both, the project cherished so long and constantly was in the nature of a bombshell.

"Oh-ho!" said Jane, recovering herself after a moment. "So me and Thomas are to be thrown out of our jobs, are we?"

Gwendolyn looked mild surprise. "But you don't *like* to be here," she reminded. "And you and Thomas wouldn't have to work any more; you could just play all the time." She smiled up at them encouragingly.

Thomas eyed Jane. "If we ain't careful," he warned in a low voice, "and let a certain party talk too much at headquarters—"

The other nodded, comprehending "I'll look sharp," she promised. "Royle will, too." Whereupon, with a forced change to gayety, and a toss of the white card aside, she lifted the cover of the box and peeked in.

It was a merry-go-round, canopied in gay stripes, and built to accommodate a party of twelve dolls. There were six deep seats, each lined with ruby plush, for as many lady dolls: There were six prancing Arab steeds—bay and chestnut and dappled gray—for an equal number of men. A small handle turned to wind up the merry-go-round. Whereupon the seats revolved gayly, the Arabs curvetted; and from the base of the stout canopy pole there sounded a merry tune.

"Oh, darlin', what a grand thing!" cried Jane, lifting Gwendolyn to stand on the rounding seat of a white-and-gold chair (a position at other times strictly forbidden). "And what a pile of money it must've cost! Why, it's as natural as the big one in the Park!"

The music and the horses appealed. Other considerations moved temporarily into the background as Gwendolyn watched and listened.

Thomas broke the string of the smaller package. "This is the Madam's present," he declared. "And I'll warrant it's a beauty!"

It proved a surprise. All paper shorn away, there stood revealed a green cabbage, topped by something fluffy and hairy and snow-white. This was a rabbit's head. And when Thomas had turned a key in the base of the cabbage, the rabbit gave a sudden hop, lifted a pair of long ears, munched at a bit of cabbage-leaf, turned his pink nose, now to the right, now to the left, and rolled two amber eyes.

"And look! Look!" shouted Jane "The eyes light up" For each was glowing as yellowly as the tiny electric bulbs on either side of Gwendolyn's dressing-table.

"Now what *more* could a little lady want!" exclaimed Thomas. "It's as wonderful, *I* say, as a wax figger."

The rabbit, with a sharp click of farewell, popped back into the cabbage. Gwendolyn got down from the chair.

"It *is* nice," she conceded. "And I'm going to ask fath-er and moth-er to come up and see it."

Neither Thomas nor Jane answered. But again he eyed the nurse, this time flashing a silent warning. After which she began to exclaim excitedly over the rabbit, while he wound up the merry-go-round. Then the ruby seats and the Arabs careened in a circle, the music played, the rabbit chewed and wriggled and rolled his luminous eyes.

An interruption came in the shape of a ring at the telephone, which stood on the small table at the head of Gwendolyn's bed. Jane answered the summons, and received the message,—a brief one. It worked, however, a noticeable change. For when Jane turned round her face was sullen.

Gwendolyn remarked the scowls. Also the fact that the moment Jane made Thomas her confidant—in an undertone—he showed plain signs of being annoyed. Gwendolyn saw the merry-go-round—cabbage and all—disappear into the large, round box without a trace of regret. So much ill-feeling on the part of nurse and man-servant undoubtedly meant that something of a decidedly pleasant nature was about to happen to herself.

It was a usual—almost a daily—occurrence for her to visit the region of the grown-ups at the dinner-hour. On such occasions she saw one, though more often both, of her parents—as well as a varying number of guests. And the privilege was one held dear.

She coveted a dearer. And her eyes roved to the larger of her two tables, where stood the tall lamp. There she ate all her meals, in the condescending company of Miss Royle. What if the telephone message meant that henceforth she was to eat *downstairs?*

Standing on one foot she waited developments, and concealed her eagerness by snapping her underlip against her teeth with one busy forefinger.

Her spirits fell when Thomas appeared with the supper-tray. And she ate with no appetite—for all that she was eating alone—alone, that is, except for Thomas, who preserved a complete and stony silence. Miss Royle had not returned. Jane had disappeared toward her room, grumbling about never having a single evening to call her own.

But at seven cheer returned with the realization that Jane was not getting ready the white-and-gold bed. Still in a very bad humor, and touched up smartly by a fresh cap and a dainty apron, the nurse put Gwendolyn into a rosebud-bordered mull frock and tied a white-satin bow atop her yellow hair.

"Where am I going, Jane?" asked Gwendolyn. (She felt certain that this was one of the nights when she was invited downstairs: She hoped—with a throb in her throat that was like the beat of a heart—that the supper just past was only afternoon tea, and that there was waiting for her at the grown-up table—in view of her newly acquired year and dignity—*an empty chair.*)

"You'll see soon enough," answered Jane, shortly.

Next, a new thought! Her father and mother had not seen her for two whole days—not since she was six. "Wonder if I show I'm not taller," she mused under her breath.

At precisely fifteen minutes to eight Jane took her by the hand. And she went down and down in the bronze cage, past the floor where were the guest chambers, past the library floor, which was where her mother and father lived, to the second floor of the great house. Here was the music-room, spacious and splendid, and the dining-room. The doors of this latter room were double. Before them the two halted.

Not only the pause at this entrance betrayed whereto they were bound, but also Jane's manner. For the nurse was holding herself erect and proper— shoulders back, chin in, heels together. Gwendolyn had often noted that upon both Jane and Thomas her parents had a curious stiffening effect.

The thought of that empty chair now forced itself uppermost. The gray eyes darkened with sudden anxiety.

"Now, Gwendolyn" whispered Jane, leaning down, "put your best foot forward." Her face had lost some of its accustomed color.

"But, Jane," whispered Gwendolyn back, "which *is* my best foot?"

Jane gave the small hand she was holding an impatient shake. "Hush your rubbishy questions," she commanded "We're goin' in!" She tapped one of the doors gently.

Gwendolyn glanced down at her daintily slippered feet. With so little time for reflecting, she could not decide which one she should put forward. Both looked equally well.

The next moment the doors swung open, and Potter, white-haired, grave and bent, stepped aside for them to pass. They crossed the threshold.

The dining-room was wide and long and lofty. Its wainscot was somberly stained. Above the wainscot, the dull tapestried walls reached to a ceiling richly panelled. The center of this dark setting was a long table, glittering with china and crystal, bright with silver and roses, and lighted by clusters of silk-shaded candles that reflected themselves upon circular table mirrors. At the far end of the table sat Gwendolyn's father, pale in his black dress-clothes, and haggard-eyed; at the near end sat her mother, pink-cheeked and pretty, with jewels about her bare throat and in her fair hair. And between the two, filling the high-backed chairs on either side of the table, were strange men and women.

Gwendolyn let go of Jane's hand and went toward her mother. Thither had gone her first glance; her second had swept the whole length of the board to her father's face. And now, without heeding any of the others, her look circled swiftly from chair to chair—searching.

Not one was empty!

The gray eyes blurred. Yet she tried to smile. Close to that dear presence, so delicately perfumed (with a haunting perfume that was a very part of her mother's charm and beauty) she halted; and curtsied—precisely as Monsieur Tellegen had taught her. And when the white-satin bow bobbed above the level of the table once more, she raised her face for a kiss.

A murmur went up and down the double row of chairs.

Gwendolyn's mother smiled radiantly. Her glance over the table was proud. "This is my little daughter's seventh birthday anniversary," she proclaimed.

To Gwendolyn the announcement was unexpected. But she was quick. Very cautiously she lifted herself on her toes—just a little.

Another buzz of comment circled the board. "*Too* sweet!" said one; and, "*Cunning!*" and "Fine child, that!"

"Now, dear," encouraged her mother.

Gwendolyn would have liked to stand still and listen to the chorus of praise. But there was something else to do.

She turned a corner of the table and started slowly along it, curtseying at each chair. As she curtsied she said nothing, only bobbed the satin bow and put out a small hand. And, "How do you do, darling!" said the ladies, and "Ah, little Miss Gwendolyn!" said the men.

The last man on that side, however, said something different. (He, she had seen at the dinner-table often.) He slipped a hand into a pocket. When it came forth, it held an oblong box. "I didn't forget that this was your birthday," he half-whispered. "Here!"—as he laid the box upon Gwendolyn's pink palm—"that's for your sweet tooth!"

Everyone was watching, the ladies beaming, the men intent and amused. But Gwendolyn was unaware both of the silence and the scrutiny. She glanced at the box. Then she looked up into the friendly eyes of the donor.

"But," she began; "—but which *is* my sweet tooth?"

There was a burst of laughter, Gwendolyn's father and mother joining in. The man who had presented the box laughed heartiest of all; then rose.

First he bowed to her mother, who acknowledged his salute graciously; next he turned to her father, whose pale face softened; last of all, he addressed her:

"Miss Gwendolyn," said he, "a toast!"

Gwendolyn looked at those bread-plates which were nearest her. There was no toast in sight, only some very nice dinner-rolls. Moreover, Potter and Thomas were not starting for the pantry, but were standing, the one behind her mother, the other behind her father, quietly listening. And what this friend of her father's had in his right hand was not anything to eat, but a delicate-stemmed glass wherein some champagne was bubbling—like amber soda-water. She was forced to conclude that he was unaccountably stupid—or only queer—or else indulging in another of those incomprehensible grown-up jokes.

He made a little speech—which she could not understand, but which elicited much laughter and polite applause; though to her it did not seem brilliant, or even interesting. Reseating himself, he patted her head.

She put the candy under her left arm, said a hasty, half-whispered Thank-you to him, went to the next high-backed chair, curtsied, bobbed the ribbon-bow and put out a hand. A pat on the head was dismissal: There was no need to wait for an answer to her question concerning her sweet tooth. Experience had taught her that whenever mirth greeted an inquiry, that inquiry was ignored.

When one whole side of the table was finished, and she turned a second corner, her father brushed her soft cheek with his lips.

"Did your dolls like the merry-go-round?" he asked kindly.

"Yes, fath—er."

"Was there something else my little girl wanted?"

Now she raised herself so far on her toes that her lips were close to his ear. For there was a lady on either side of him. And both were plainly listening.

"If—if you'd come up and make it go," she said, almost whispering.

He nodded energetically.

She went behind his chair. Thomas was in wait there still. Down here he seemed to raise a wall of aloofness between himself and her, to wear a magnificent air, all cold and haughty, that was quite foreign to the nursery. As she passed him, she dimpled up at him saucily. But it failed to slack the starchy tenseness of his visage.

She turned another corner and curtsied her way along the opposite side of the table. On this side were precisely as many high-backed chairs as on the other. And now, "You *adorable* child!" cried the ladies, and "Haw! Haw! Don't the rest of us get a smile?" said the men.

When all the curtseying was over, and the last corner was turned, she paused. "And what is my daughter going to say about the rabbit in the cabbage?" asked her mother.

There was a man seated on either hand. Gwendolyn gave each a quick glance. At Johnnie Blake's she had been often alone with her father and mother during that one glorious week. But in town her little confidences, for the most part, had to be made in just this way—under the eye of listening guests and servants, in a low voice.

"I like the rabbit," she answered, "but my Puffy Bear was nicer, only he got old and shabby, and so—"

At this point Jane took one quick step forward.

"But if you'd come up to the nursery soon," Gwendolyn hastened to add. "*Would* you, moth—er?"

"Yes, indeed, dear."

Gwendolyn went up to Jane, who was waiting, rooted and rigid, close by. The reddish eyes of the nurse-maid fairly bulged with importance. Her lips were sealed primly. Her face was so pale that every freckle she had stood forth clearly. How strangely—even direly—the great dining-room affected *her*—who was so at ease in the nursery! No smile, no wink, no remark, either lively or sensible, ever melted the ice of *her* countenance. And it was with a look almost akin to pity that Gwendolyn held out a hand.

Jane took it with a great show of affection. Then once more Potter swung wide the double doors.

Gwendolyn turned her head for a last glimpse of her father, sitting, grave and haggard, at the far end of the table; at her beautiful, jeweled mother; at the double line of high-backed chairs that showed, now a man's stern black-and-white, next the gayer colors of a woman's dress; at the clustered lights; the glitter; the roses—

Then the doors closed, making faint the din of chatter and laughter. And the bronze cage carried Gwendolyn up and up.

CHAPTER III

There was a high wind blowing, and the newly washed garments hanging on the roofs of nearby buildings were writhing and twisting violently, and tugging at the long swagging clothes-lines. Gwendolyn, watching from the side window of the nursery, pretended that the garments were so many tortured creatures, vainly struggling to be free. And she wished that two or three of the whitest and prettiest might loose their hold and go flying away —across the crescent of the Drive and the wide river—to liberty and happiness in the forest beyond.

Among the flapping lines walked maids—fully a score of them. Some were taking down wash that was dry and stuffing it into baskets. Others were busy hanging up limp pieces, first giving them a vigorous shake; then putting a small portion of each over the line and pinching all securely into place with huge wooden pins.

It seemed cruel.

Yet the faces of the maids were kind—kinder than the faces of Miss Royle and Jane and Thomas. Behind Gwendolyn the heavy brocade curtains hung touching. She parted them to make sure that she was alone in the nursery. After which she raised the window—just a trifle. The roofs that were white with laundry were not those directly across from the nursery, but over-looked the next street. Nevertheless, with the window up, Gwendolyn could hear the crack and snap of the whipping garments, and an indistinct chorus of cheery voices. One maid was singing a lilting tune. The rest were chattering back and forth. With all her heart Gwendolyn envied them— envied their freedom, and the fact that they were indisputably grown-up. And she decided that, later on, when she was as big and strong, she would be a laundry-maid and run about on just such level roofs, joyously hanging up wash.

Presently she raised the window a trifle more, so that the lower sill was above her head. Then, "*Hoo*-hoo-oo-oo!" she piped in her clear voice.

A maid heard her, and pointed her out to another. Soon a number were looking her way. They smiled at her, too, Gwendolyn smiled in return, and nodded. At that, one of a group snatched up a square of white cloth and waved it. Instantly Gwendolyn waved back.

One by one the maids went. Then Gwendolyn suddenly recalled why she was waiting alone—while Miss Royle and Jane made themselves extra neat in their respective rooms; why she herself was dressed with such unusual care—in a pink muslin, white silk stockings, and black patent-leather pumps, the whole crowned by a pink-satin hair-bow. With the remembrance, the pretend-game was forgotten utterly: The lines of limp, white creatures on the roofs flung their tortured shapes about unheeded.

At bed-time the previous evening Potter had telephoned that Madam would pay a morning visit to the nursery. The thought had kept Gwendolyn awake for a while, smiling into the dark, kissing her own hands for very happiness; it had made her heart beat wildly, too. For she reviewed all the things she intended broaching to her mother—about eating at the grown-up table, and not having a nurse any more, and going to day-school.

Contrary to a secret plan of action, she slept late. At breakfast, excitement took away her appetite. And throughout the study-hour that followed, her eyes read, and her lips repeated aloud, several pages of standard literature for juveniles that her busy brain did not comprehend. Yet now as she waited behind the rose hangings for the supreme moment, she felt, strangely enough, no impatience. With three to attend her, privacy was not a common privilege, and, therefore, prized. She fell to inspecting the row of houses across the way—in search for other strange but friendly faces.

There were exactly twelve houses opposite. The corner one farthest from the river she called the gray-haired house. An old lady lived there who knitted bright worsted; also a fat old gentleman in a gay skull-cap who showed much attention to a long-leaved rubber-plant that flourished behind the glass of the street door. Gwendolyn leaned out, chin on palm, to canvass the quaintly curtained windows—none of which at the moment framed a venerable head. Next the gray-haired house there had been—up to a recent date—a vacant lot walled off from the sidewalk by a high, broad bill-board. Now a pit yawned where formerly was the vacant space. And instead of the fascinating pictures that decorated the bill-board (one week a baby, rosy, dimpled and laughing; the next some huge lettering elaborately combined with a floral design; the next a mammoth bottle, red and beautiful, and flanked by a single gleaming word: "Catsup") there towered—above street and pit, and even above the chimneys of the gray-haired house—the naked girders of a new steel structure.

The girders were black, but rusted to a brick-color in patches and streaks. They were so riveted together that through them could be seen small, regular spots of light. Later on, as Gwendolyn knew, floors and windowed walls and a tin top would be fitted to the framework. And what was now a skeleton would be another house!

Directly opposite the nursery, on that part of the side street which sloped, were ten narrow houses, each four stories high, each with brown-stone fronts and brown-stone steps, each topped by a large chimney and a small chimney. In every detail these ten houses were precisely alike. Jane, for some unaccountable reason, referred to them as private dwellings. But since the roof of the second brown-stone house was just a foot lower than the roof of the first, the third roof just a foot lower than the roof of the second, and so on to the very tenth and last, Gwendolyn called these ten the step-houses.

The step-houses were seldom interesting. As Gwendolyn's glances traveled now from brown-stone front to brown-stone front, not one presented even the relief of a visiting post-man.

Her progress down the line of step-houses brought her by degrees to the brick house on the Drive—a large vine-covered house, the wide entrance of which was toward the river. And no sooner had she given it one quick glance than she uttered a little shout of pleased surprise. The brick-house people were back!

All the shades were up. There was smoke rising from one of the four tall chimneys. And even as Gwendolyn gazed, all absorbed interest, the net curtains at an upper window were suddenly drawn aside and a face looked out.

It was a face that Gwendolyn had never seen before in the brick house. But though it was strange, it was entirely friendly. For as Gwendolyn smiled it a greeting, it smiled her a greeting back!

She was a nurse-maid—so much was evident from the fact that she wore a cap. But it was also plain that her duties differed in some way from Jane's. For her cap was different—shaped like a sugar-bowl turned upside-down; hollow, and white, and marred by no flying strings.

And she was not a red-haired nurse-maid. Her hair was almost as fair as Gwendolyn's own, and it framed her face in a score of saucy wisps and curls. Her face was pretty—full and rosy, like the face of Gwendolyn's French doll. Also it seemed certain—even at such a distance—that she had no freckles. Gwendolyn waved both hands at her. She threw a kiss back.

"Oh, thank you!" cried Gwendolyn, out loud. She threw kisses with alternating finger-tips.

The nurse-maid shook the curtains at her. Then—they fell into place. She was gone.

Gwendolyn sighed.

The next moment she heard voices in the direction of the hall—first, Thomas's; next, a woman's—a strange one this. Disappointed, she turned to face the screening curtains. But she was in no mood to make herself agreeable to visiting friends of Miss Royle's—and who else could this be?

She decided to remain quietly in seclusion; to emerge for no one except her mother.

A door opened. A heavy step advanced, followed by the murmur of trailing skirts upon carpet. Then Thomas spoke—his tone that full and measured one employed, not to the governess, to Jane, to herself, or to any other common mortal, but to Potter, to her father and mother, and to guests. "This is Miss Gwendolyn's nursery," he announced.

Beyond the curtains were persons of importance!

She shrank against the window, taking care not to stir the brocade.

"We will wait here,"—the voice was clear, musical.

"Thank you." Thomas's heavy step retreated. A door closed.

There was a moment of perfect stillness. Then that musical voice began again:

"Where do you suppose that young one is?"

A second voice rippled out a low laugh.

Gwendolyn laughed too,—silently, her face against the glass. The fat old gentleman in the gray-haired house chanced to be looking in her direction. He caught the broad smile and joined in.

"In the school-room likely,"—it was the first speaker, answering her own inquiry—"getting stuffed."

Stuffed! Gwendolyn could appreciate *that*. She choked back a giggle with one small hand.

Someone else thought the declaration amusing, for there was another well-bred ripple; then once more that murmur of trailing skirts, going toward the window-seat; going the opposite way also, as if one of the two was making a circuit of the room.

Presently, "Just look at this dressing-table, Louise! Fancy such a piece of furniture for a *child!* Ridiculous!"

Gwendolyn cocked her yellow head to one side—after the manner of her canary.

"Bad taste." Louise joined her companion. "*Crystal,* if you please! Must've cost a fabulous sum."

One or two articles were moved on the dresser. Then, "Poor little girl!" observed the other woman. "Rich, but—"

Gwendolyn puckered her brows gravely. Was the speaker referring to *her?* Clasping her hands tight, she leaned forward a little, straining to catch every syllable. As a rule when gossip or criticism was talked in her hearing, it was insured against being understood by the use of strange terms, spellings, winks, nods, shrugs, or sudden stops at the most important point. But now, with herself hidden, was there not a likelihood of plain speech?

It came.

The voice went on: "This is the first time you've met the mother, isn't it?"

"I think so,"—indifferently. "Who is she, anyhow?"

"*Nobody.*"

Gwendolyn stared.

"Nobody at all—*absolutely*. You know, they say—" She paused for emphasis.

Now, Gwendolyn's eyes grew suddenly round; her lips parted in surprise. *They* again!

"Yes?" encouraged Louise.

Lower—"They say she was just an ordinary country girl, pretty, and horribly poor, with a fair education, but no culture to speak of. She met him; he had money and fell in love with her; she married him. And, oh, *then!*" She chuckled.

"Made the money fly?"

The two were coming to settle themselves in chairs close to the side window.

"Not exactly. Haven't you heard what's the matter with her?"

Gwendolyn's face paled a little. There was something the matter with her mother?—her dear, beautiful, young mother! The clasped hands were pressed to her breast.

"Ambitious?" hazarded Louise, confidently.

"It's no secret. Everybody's laughing at her,—at the rebuffs she takes; the money she gives to charity (wedges, you understand); the quantities of dresses she buys; the way she slaps on the jewels. She's got the society bee in her bonnet!"

Gwendolyn caught her breath. *The society bee in her bonnet?*

"Ah!" breathed Louise, as if comprehending. Then, "Dear! dear!"

"She *talks* nothing else. She *hears* nothing else. She *sees* nothing else."

"Bad as that?"

"Goes wherever she can shove in—subscription lectures and musicales, hospital teas, Christmas bazars. And she benches her Poms; has boxes at the Horse Show and the Opera; gives gold-plate dinners, and Heaven knows what!"

"Ha! ha! *You* haven't boosted her, dear?"

"Not a bit of it! Make a point of never being seen *any*where with her."

"And he?"

Gwendolyn swallowed. *He* was her father.

"Well, it has kept the poor fellow in harness all the time, of course. You should have seen him when he *first* came to town—straight and boyish, and *very* handsome. (You know the type.) He's changed! Burns his candles at both ends."

"Hm!"

Gwendolyn blinked with the effort of making mental notes.

"You haven't heard the latest about him?"

"Trying to make some Club?"

Whispering—"On the edge of a *crash*."

"Who told you?"

"Oh, a little bird."

Up came both palms to cover Gwendolyn's mouth. But not to smother mirth. A startled cry had all but escaped her. A little bird! She knew of that bird! He had told things against *her*—true things more often than not—to Jane and Miss Royle. And now here he was chattering about her father!

"It's the usual story," commented Louise calmly, "with these *nouveaux riches*."

"Sh!" A moment of stillness, as if both were listening. Then, "*Sprechen Sie Deutsch?*"

"I—er—read it fairly well."

"*Parlez-vous Francais?*"

"*Oh, oui! Oui!*"

"*Allors.*" And there followed, in undertones, a short, spirited conversation in the Gallic.

Gwendolyn made a silent resolution to devote more time and thought to the peevish and staccato instruction of Miss Du Bois.

The two were interrupted by a light, quick step outside. Again the hall door opened.

"Oh, you'll pardon my having to desert you, *won't* you?" It was Gwendolyn's mother. "I didn't intend being so long."

Gwendolyn half-started forward, then stopped.

"Why, of course!"—with sounds of rising.

"*Cer*tainly!"

"Differences below stairs, I find, require prompt action."

"I fancy you have oceans of executive ability," declared Louise, warmly. "That Orphans' Home affair—I hear you managed it tre*men*dously!"

"No! No!"

"Really, my dear,"—it was the other woman—"to be *quite* frank, we must confess that we haven't missed you! We've been enjoying our glimpse of the nursery."

"It's simply *lovely!*" cried Louise.

"And what a perfectly sweet dressing-table!"

"Have you seen my little daughter?—Thomas!"

"Yes, Madam."

"There's a draught coming from somewhere—"

"It's the side window, Madam."

Instinctively Gwendolyn flattened herself against the wood-work at her back.

Three or four steps brought Thomas across the floor. Then his two big hands appeared high up on the hangings. The next moment, the hands parted, sweeping the curtains with them.

To escape detection was impossible. A quick thought made Gwendolyn raise a face upon which was a forced expression that bore only a faint resemblance to a smile.

"Boo!" she said, jumping out at him.

Startled, he fell back. "Why, Miss Gwendolyn!"

"Gwendolyn?" repeated her mother, surprised. "Why, what were you doing there, darling?"

"*Gwendolyn!*"—this in a faint gasp from both visitors.

Gwendolyn came slowly forward. She did not raise her eyes; only curtsied.

"So *this* is your little daughter!" A gloved hand was reached out, and Gwendolyn was drawn forward. "How *cunning!*"

Gwendolyn recognized the voice of Louise. Now, she looked up. And saw a pleasant face, young, but not so pretty as her mother's. She shook hands bashfully. Then shook again with an older woman, whose plain countenance was dimly familiar. After which, giving a sudden little bound, and putting up eager arms, she was caught to her mother.

"My baby!"

"*Moth-er!*"

Cheek caressed cheek.

"She's six, isn't she, my dear?" asked the plain, elderly one.

"Oh, she's seven." A soft hand stroked the yellow hair.

"As much as that? Really?"

The inference was not lost upon Gwendolyn. She tightened her embrace. And turning her head on her mother's breast, looked frank resentment.

The visitors were not watching her. They were exchanging glances—and smiles, faint and uneasy. Slowly now they began to move toward the hall door, which stood open. Beside it, waiting with an impressive air, was Miss Royle.

"I think we must go, Louise."

"Oh, we must,"—quickly. "Dear me! I'd almost forgot! We've promised to lunch with one or two people down-town."

"I wish you were lunching here," said Gwendolyn's mother. She freed herself gently from the clinging arms and followed the two. "Miss Royle, will you take Gwendolyn?"

As the governess promptly advanced, with a half-bow, and a set smile that was like a grimace, Gwendolyn raised a face tense with earnestness. Until half an hour before, her whole concern had been for herself. But now! To fail to grow up, to have her long-cherished hopes come short of fulfillment —that was *one* thing. To know that her mother and father had real and serious troubles of their own, that was another!

"Oh, moth-er! Don't *you* go!"

"Mother must tell the ladies good-by."

"What touching affection!" It was the elder of the visiting pair.

Miss Royle assented with a simper.

"Will you come back?" urged Gwendolyn, dropping her voice. "Oh, I want to see you"—darting a look sidewise—"all by myself."

There was a wheel and a flutter at the door—another silent exchange of comment, question and exclamation, all mingled eloquently. Then Louise swept back.

"What a bright child!" she enthused. "Does she speak French?"

"She is acquiring two tongues at present," answered Gwendolyn's mother proudly, "—French and German."

"*Splendid!*" It was the elder woman. "I think every little girl should have those. And later on, I suppose, Greek and Latin?"

"I've thought of Spanish and Italian."

"*Eventually,*" informed Miss Royle, with a conscious, sinuous shift from foot to foot, "Gwendolyn will have *seven* tongues at her command."

"How *chic!*" Once more the gloved hand was extended—to pat the pink-satin hair-bow.

Gwendolyn accepted the pat stolidly. Her eyes were fixed on her mother's face.

Now, the elder of the strangers drew closer. "I wonder," she began, addressing her hostess with almost a coy air, "if we could induce *you* to take lunch with us down-town. Wouldn't that be jolly, Louise?"—turning.

"*Awfully* jolly!"

"*Do* come!"

"Oh, *do!*"

"Moth-er!"

Gwendolyn's mother looked down. A sudden color was mounting to her cheeks. Her eyes shone.

"We-e-ell," she said, with rising inflection.

It was acceptance.

Gwendolyn stepped back the pink muslin in a nervous grasp at either side. "Oh, *won't* you stay?" she half-whispered.

"Mother'll see you at dinnertime, darling. Tell Jane, Miss Royle."

A bow.

Louise led the way quickly, followed by the elderly lady. Gwendolyn's mother came last. A bronze gate slid between the three and Gwendolyn, watching them go. The cage lowered noiselessly, with a last glimpse of upturned faces and waving hands.

Gwendolyn, lips pouting, crossed toward the school-room door. The door was slightly ajar. She gave it a smart pull.

A kneeling figure rose from behind it. It was Jane, who greeted her with a nervous, and somewhat apprehensive grin.

"I was waitin' to jump out at Miss Royle and give her a scare when she'd come through," she explained.

Gwendolyn said nothing.

CHAPTER IV

It was a morning abounding in unexpected good fortune. For one thing, Miss Royle was indisposed—to an extent that was fully convincing—and was lying down, brows swathed by a towel, in her own room; for another, the bursting of a hot-water pipe on the same floor as the nursery required the prompt attention of a man in a greasy cap and Johnnie Blake overalls, who, as he hammered and soldered and coupled lengths of piping with his wrench, discussed various grown-up topics in a loud voice with Jane, thus levying on *her* attention. Miss Royle's temporary incapacity set aside the program of study usual to each forenoon; and Jane's suddenly aroused interest in plumbing made the canceling of that day's riding-lesson seem advisable. It was Thomas who telephoned the postponement. And Gwendolyn found herself granted some little time to herself.

But she was not playing any of the games she loved—the absorbing pretend-games with which she occupied herself on just such rare occasions. Her own pleasure, her own disappointment, too,—these were entirely put aside in a concern touching weightier matters. Slippers upheld by a hassock, and slender pink-frocked figure bent across the edge of the school-room table, she had each elbow firmly planted on a page of the wide-open, dictionary.

At all times the volume was beguiling—this in spite of the fact that the square of black-board always carried along its top, in glaring chalk, the irritating reminder: *Use Your Dictionary!* There was diversion in turning the leaves at random (blissfully ignoring the while any white list that might be inscribed down the whole of the board) to chance upon big, strange words.

But the word she was now poring over was a small one. "B-double-e," she spelled; "Bee: a so-cial hon-ey-gath-er-ing in-sect."

She pondered the definition with wrinkled forehead and worried eye. "Social"—the word seemed vaguely linked with that other word, "Society", which she had so fortunately overheard. But what of the remainder of that visitor's never-to-be-forgotten declaration of scorn? For the definition had absolutely nothing to say about any *bonnet*.

She was shoving the pages forward with an impatient damp thumb in her search for Bonnet, when Thomas entered, slipping in around the edge of the hall door on soft foot—with a covert peek nursery-ward that was designed to lend significance to his coming. His countenance, which on occasion could be so rigorously sober, was fairly askew with a smile.

Gwendolyn stood up straight on the hassock to look at him. And at first glance divined that something—probably in the nature of an edible—might be expected. For the breast-pocket of his liveried coat bulged promisingly.

"Hello!" he saluted, tiptoeing genially across the room.

"Hello!" she returned noncommittally.

Near the table, he reached into the bulging pocket and drew out a small Manila bag. The bag was partly open at the top. He tipped his head to direct one black eye upon its contents.

"Say, Miss Gwendolyn," he began, "*you* like old Thomas, don't you?"

Gwendolyn's nostrils widened and quivered, receiving the tempting fragrance of fresh-roasted peanuts. At the same time, her eyes lit with glad surprise. Since her seventh anniversary, she had noted a vast change for the better in the attitude of Miss Royle, Thomas and Jane; where, previous to the birthday, it had seemed the main purpose of the trio (if not the duty) to circumvent her at every turn—to which end, each had a method that was unique: the first commanded; the second threatened; Thomas employed sarcasm or bribery. But now this wave of thoughtfulness, generosity and smooth speech!—marking a very era in the history of the nursery. Here was fresh evidence that it was *continuing*.

Yet—was it not too good to last?

"Why, ye-e-es," she answered, more than half guessing that this time bribery was in the air.

But the fragrant bag resolved itself into a friendly offering. Thomas let it drop to the table.

Casting her last doubt aside, Gwendolyn caught it up eagerly. Miss Royle never permitted her to eat peanuts, which lent to them all the charm of the forbidden. She cracked a pod; and fell to crunching merrily.

"And you wouldn't like to see me go away, *would* you now," went on Thomas.

Her mouth being crammed, she shook her head cordially.

"Ah! I thought so!" He tore the bag down the side so that she could more easily get at its store. Then, leaning down confidentially, and pointing a teasing finger at her, "Ha! Ha! Who was it got caught spyin' yesterday?"

The small jaws ceased grinding. She lifted her eyes. Their gray was suddenly clouded—remembering what, for a moment, her joy in the peanuts had blotted out. "But I *wasn't* spying," she denied earnestly.

"Then what *was* you doin'?—still as mice behind them curtains."

The mist cleared. Her face sunned over once more. "I was waving at the nurse in the brick house," she explained.

At that, up went Thomas's head. His mouth opened. His ears grew red. "The nurse in the brick house!" he repeated softly.

"The one with the curly hair," went on Gwendolyn, cracking more pods.

Thomas turned his face toward the side window of the school-room. Through it could be seen the chimneys of the brick house. He smacked his lips.

"You like peanuts, too," said Gwendolyn. She proffered the bag.

He ignored it. His look was dreamy. "There's a fine Pomeranian at the brick house," he remarked.

"It was the first time I'd ever seen her," said Gwendolyn, with the nurse still in mind. "Doesn't she smile nice!"

Now, Thomas waxed enthusiastic. "And she's a lot prettier close to," he declared, "than she is with a street between. Ah, you ought—"

That moment, Jane entered, fairly darting in.

"Here!" she called sharply to Gwendolyn. "What're you eatin'?"

"Peanuts, Jane,"—perfect frankness being the rule when concealment was not possible.

Jane came over. "And where'd you git 'em?" she demanded, promptly seizing the bag as contraband.

"Thomas."

Sudden suspicion flamed in Jane's red glance. "Oh, you must've did Thomas a *grand* turn," she observed.

Thomas shifted from foot to foot. "I was—er—um—just tellin' Miss Gwendolyn"—he winked significantly—"that she wouldn't like to lose us."

"So?" said Jane, still sceptical. Then to Gwendolyn, after a moment's reflection. "Let me close up your dictionary for you, pettie. Jane never likes to see one of your fine books lyin' open that way. It might put a strain on the back."

Emboldened by that cooing tone, Gwendolyn eyed the Manila bag covetously. "I didn't eat many," she asserted, gently argumentative.

"Oh, a peanut or two won't hurt you, lovie," answered Jane, kneeling to present the bag. Then drawing the pink-frocked figure close, "And you *didn't* tell him what them two ladies had to say?"

"No." It was decisive, "I told him about—"

"I didn't ask her," interrupted Thomas. "No; I talked about how she loves us. And a-course, she does.... Jane, ain't it near twelve?"

But Gwendolyn had no mind to be held as a tattler. "I told him," she continued, husking peanuts busily, "about the nurse-maid at the brick house."

Jane sat back.

"Ah?" She flashed a glance at Thomas, still shifting about uneasily mid-way between table and door. Then, "What *about* the nurse-maid, dearie?"

It was Gwendolyn's turn to wax enthusiastic. "Oh, she has *such* sweet hair!" she exclaimed. "And she smiles nice!"

Jealousy hardened the freckled visage of the kneeling Jane. "And she's taken with you, I suppose," said she.

"She threw me kisses," recounted Gwendolyn, crunching happily the while. "And, oh, Jane, some day may I go over to the brick house?"

"Some day you may—*not*."

Gwendolyn recognized the sudden change to belligerence; and foreseeing a possible loss of the peanuts, commenced to eat more rapidly. "Well, then," she persisted, "she could come over here."

Jane stared. "What do you mean?" she demanded crossly. "And don't you go botherin' your poor father and mother about this strange woman. Do you *hear?*"

"But she takes care of a rich little girl. I *know*—'cause there are bars on the basement windows. And Thomas says—"

"Oh, *come*" broke in Thomas, urging Jane hallward with a nervous jerk of the head.

"Ah!" Now complete understanding brought Jane to her feet. She fixed Thomas with blazing eyes. "And *what* does Thomas say, darlin'?"

Thomas waited. His ears were a dead white.

"There's a Pomeranian at the brick house," went on Gwendolyn, "and the pretty nurse takes it out to walk. And—"

"And Thomas is a-walkin' our Poms at the same time." Jane was breathing hard.

"And he says she's lots prettier close to—"

A bell rang sharply. Thomas sprang away. With a gurgle, Jane flounced after.

The next moment Gwendolyn, from the hassock—upon which she had settled in comfort—heard a wrangle of voices: First, Jane's shrill accusing, "It was *you* put it into her head!—to come—and take my place from under me—and the food out of my very mouth—and break my hear-r-r-rt!" Next, Thomas's sonorous, "Stuff and fiddle-sticks!" then sounds of lamentation, and the slamming of a door.

The last peanut was eaten. As Gwendolyn searched out some few remaining bits from the crevices of the bag, she shook her yellow hair hopelessly. Truly there was no fathoming grown-ups!

The morning which had begun so propitiously ended in gloom. At the noon dinner, Thomas looked harassed. He had set the table for one. That single plate, as well as the empty arm-chair so popular with Jane, emphasized the infestivity. As for the heavy curtains at the side window, which—as near as Gwendolyn could puzzle it out—were the cause of the late unpleasantness, these were closely drawn.

Having already eaten heartily, Gwendolyn had little appetite. Furthermore, again she was turning over and over the direful statements made concerning her parents. She employed the dinner-hour in formulating a plan that was simple but daring—one that would bring quick enlightenment concerning the things that worried. Miss Royle was still indisposed. Jane was locked in her own room, from which issued an occasional low bellow. When Thomas, too, was out of the way—gone pantry-ward with tray held aloft—she would carry it out. It called for no great amount of time: no searching of the dictionary. She would close all doors softly; then fly to the telephone—*and call up her father*.

There were times when Thomas—as well as the two others—seemed to possess the power of divination. And during the whole of the dinner his manner showed distinct apprehension. The meal concluded, even to the use of the finger-bowl, and all dishes disposed upon the tray, he hung about, puttering with the table, picking up crumbs and pins, dusting this article and that with a napkin,—all the while working his lips with silent speech, and drawing down and lifting his black eye-brows menacingly.

Meanwhile, Gwendolyn fretted. But found some small diversion in standing before the pier glass, at which, between the shining rows of her teeth, she thrust out a tip of scarlet. She was thinking about the discussion anent tongues held by her mother and the two visitors.

"Seven," she murmured, and viewed the greater part of her own tongue thoughtfully; "*seven*."

The afternoon was a French-and-music afternoon. Directly after dinner might be expected the Gallic teacher—undesired at any hour. Thomas puttered and frowned until a light tap announced her arrival. Then quickly handed Gwendolyn over to her company.

Mademoiselle Du Bois was short and spare. And these defects she emphasized by means of a wide hat and a long feather boa. She led Gwendolyn to the school-room. There she settled down in a low chair, opened a black reticule, took out a thick, closely written letter, and fell to reading.

Gwendolyn amused herself by experimenting with the boa, which she festooned, now over one shoulder, now over the other. "Mademoiselle," she began, "what kind of a bird owned these feathers?"

"Dear me, Mees Gwendolyn," chided Mademoiselle, irritably (she spoke with much precision and only a slight accent), "how you talk!"

Talk—the word was a cue! Why not make certain inquiries of Mademoiselle?

"But do little *birds* ever talk?" returned Gwendolyn, undaunted. The boa was thin at one point. She tied a knot in it. "And which little bird is it that tells things to—to people?" Then, more to herself than to Mademoiselle, who was still deep in her letter, "I shouldn't wonder if it wasn't the little bird that's in the cuckoo clock, though—"

"*Ma foil!*" exclaimed Mademoiselle. She seized an end of the boa and drew Gwendolyn to her knee. "You make ze head buzz. Come!" She reached for a book on the school-room table. "*Attendez!*"

"Mademoiselle," persisted Gwendolyn, twining and untwining, "if I do my French fast will you tell me something? What does *nouveaux riches* mean?"

"*Nouveaux riches*," said Mademoiselle, "is not on ziss page. *Attendez-vous!*"

Miss Brown followed Mademoiselle Du Bois, the one coming upon the heels of the other; so that a loud *crescendo* from the nursery, announcing the arrival of the music-teacher, drowned the last paragraph of French.

To Gwendolyn an interruption at any time was welcome. This day it was doubly so. She had learned nothing from Mademoiselle. But Miss Brown— She made toward the nursery, doing her newest dance step.

Miss Brown was stocky, with a firm tread and an eye of decision. As Gwendolyn appeared, she was seated at the piano, her face raised (as if she were seeking out some spot on the ceiling), and her solid frame swaying from side to side in the ecstasy of performance. Up and down the key-board of the instrument her plump hands galloped.

Gwendolyn paused beside the piano-seat. The air was vibrant with melody. The lifted face, the rocking, the ardent touch—all these inspired hope. The gray eyes were wide with eagerness. Each corner of the rosy mouth was upturned.

The resounding notes of a march ended with a bang. Miss Brown straightened—got to her feet—smiled down.

That smile gave Gwendolyn renewed encouragement. They were alone. She stood on tiptoe. "Miss Brown," she began, "did you ever hear of a—a bee that some ladies carry in a—"

Miss Brown's smile of greeting went. "Now, Gwendolyn," she interrupted severely, "are you going to begin your usual silly, silly questions?"

Gwendolyn fell back a step. "But I didn't ask you a silly question day before yesterday," she plead. "I just wanted to know how *any*body could call my German teacher Miss *French*."

"Take your place, if you please," bade Miss Brown curtly, "and don't waste my time." She pointed a stubby finger at the piano-seat.

Gwendolyn climbed up, her cheeks scarlet with wounded dignity, her breast heaving with a rancor she dared not express. "Do I have to play that old piece?" she asked.

"You must,"—with rising inflection.

"Up at Johnnie Blake's it sounded nice. 'Cause my moth-er—"

"Ready!" Miss Brown set the metronome to *tick-tocking*. Then she consulted a watch.

Gwendolyn raised one hand to her face, and gulped.

"Come! Come! Put your fingers on the keys."

"But my cheek itches."

"Get your position, I say."

Gwendolyn struck a spiritless chord.

Miss Brown gone, Gwendolyn sought the long window-seat and curled up among its cushions—at the side which commanded the best view of the General. Straight before that martial figure, on the bridle-path, a man with a dump-cart and a shaggy-footed horse was picking up leaves. He used a shovel. And each time he raised it to shoulder-height and emptied it into his cart, a few of the leaves went whirling away out of reach—like frightened butterflies. But she had no time to pretend anything of the kind. A new and a better plan!—this was what she must prepare. For—heart beating, hands trembling from haste—she had *tried* the telephone—*and found it dead to every Hello!*

But she was not discouraged. She was only balked.

The talking bird, the bee her mother kept in a bonnet, her father's harness, and the candles that burned at both ends—if she had *only* known about them that evening of her seventh anniversary! Ignoring Miss Royle's oft-repeated lesson that "Nice little girls do not ask questions," or "worry father and mother," how easy it would have been to say, "Fath-er, what little bird tells things about you?" and, "Moth-er, have you *really* got a bee in your bonnet?"

But—the questions could still be asked. She was balked only temporarily.

She got down and crossed the room to the white-and-gold writing-desk. Two photographs in silver frames stood upon it, flanking the rose-embossed calendar at either side. She took them down, one at a time, and looked at them earnestly.

The first was of her mother, taken long, long ago, before Gwendolyn was born. The oval face was delicately lovely and girlish. The mouth curved in a smile that was tender and sweet.

The second photograph showed a clean-shaven, boyish young man in a rough business-suit—this was her father, when he first came to the city. His lips were set together firmly, almost determinedly. But his face was unlined, his dark eyes were full of laughter.

Despite all the well-remembered commands Miss Royle had issued; despite Jane's oft-repeated threats and Thomas's warnings, [and putting aside, too, any thought of what punishment might follow her daring] Gwendolyn now made a firm resolution: *To see at least one of her parents immediately and alone.*

As she set the photographs back in their places, she lifted each to kiss it. She kissed the smiling lips of the one, the laughing eyes of the other.

CHAPTER V

The crescent of the Drive, never without its pageant; the broad river thronged with craft; the high forest-fringed precipice and the houses that could be glimpsed beyond—all these played their part in Gwendolyn's pretend-games. She crowded the Drive with the soldiers of the General, rank upon rank of marching men whom he reviewed with pride, while his great bronze steed pranced tirelessly; and she, a swordless Joan of Arc in a three-cornered hat and smartly-tailored habit, pranced close beside to share all honors from the wide back of her own mettlesome war-horse.

As for the river vessels, she took long pretend-journeys upon them—every detail of which she carefully carried out. The companions selected were those smiling friends that appeared at neighboring windows; or she chose hearty, happy laundresses from the roofs; adding, by way of variety, some small, bashful acquaintances made at the dancing-school of Monsieur Tellegen.

But more often, imagining herself a Princess, and the nursery a prison-tower from the loop-holes of which she viewed the great, free world, she liked to people the boats out of stories that Potter had told her on rare, but happy, occasions. A prosaic down-traveling steamer became the wonderful ship of Ulysses, his seamen bound to smokestacks and railing, his prow pointed for the ocean whereinto the River crammed its deep flood. A smaller boat, smoking its way up-stream, changed into the fabled bark of a man by the name of Jason, and at the bow of this Argo sat Johnnie Blake, fish-pole over the side, feet dangling, line trailing, and a silvery trout spinning at the hook. A third boat, smaller still, and driven forward by oars, bore a sad, level-lying, white-clad figure—Elaine, dead through the plotting of cruel servants, and now rowed by the hoary dumb toward a peaceful mooring at the foot of some far timbered slope.

In each of the houses across the wide river, she often established a pretend-home. Her father was with her always; her mother, too,—in a silken gown, with a jeweled chaplet on her head. But her household was always blissfully free of those whose chief design it was to thwart and terrify her—Miss Royle, Jane, Thomas; her teachers [as a body]; also, Policemen, Doctors and Bears. Old Potter was, of course, the pretend-butler. And Rosa, notwithstanding the fact that she had once been, while at Johnnie Blake's, the herald of a hated bed-time went as maid.

Gwendolyn had often secretly coveted the Superintendent's residence in the Park (so that, instead of straggling along a concrete pavement at rare intervals, held captive by the hand that was in Jane's, she might always have the right to race willy-nilly across the grass—chase the tame squirrels to shelter—*even climb a tree*). But more earnestly did she covet a house beyond the precipice. Were there not trees there? and rocks? Without doubt there were Johnnie Blake glades as well—glades bright with flowers, and green with lacy ferns. For of these glades Gwendolyn had received proof: Following a sprinkle on a cool day, a light west wind brought a butterfly against a pane of the front window. When Gwendolyn raised the sash, the butterfly fluttered in, throwing off a jeweled drop as he came and alighted upon the dull rose and green of a flower in the border of the nursery rug. His wings were flat together and he was tipped to one side, like a skiff with tinted sails. But when the sails were dry, and parted once more, and sunlight had replaced shower, he launched forth from the pink landing-place of Gwendolyn's palm—and sped away and away, due west!

But the view from the *side* window!

Beyond the line of step-houses, and beyond the buildings where the maids hung their wash, were roofs. They seemed to touch, to have no streets between them anywhere. They reached as far as Gwendolyn could see. They were all heights, all shapes, all varieties as to tops—some being level, others coming to a point at one corner, a few ending in a tower. One tower, which was square, and on the outer-most edge of the roofs, had a clock in its summit. When night settled, a light sprang up behind the clock—a great, round light that was like a single shining eye.

She did not know the proper name for all those acres of roof. But Jane called them Down-Town.

At all times they were fascinating. Of a winter's day the snow whitened them into beauty. The rain washed them with its slanting down-pour till their metal sheeting glistened as brightly as the sides of the General's horse. The sea-fog, advanced by the wind, blotted out all but the nearest, wrapped these in torn shrouds, and heaped itself about the dun-breathed chimneys like the smoke of a hundred fires.

She loved the roofs far more than Drive or River or wooded expanse; more because they meant so much—and that without her having to do much pretending. For across them, in some building which no one had ever pointed out to her, in a street through which she had never driven, was her father's office!

She herself often selected the building he was in, placing him first in one great structure, then in another. Whenever a new one rose, as it often did, there she promptly moved his office. Once for a whole week he worked directly under the great glowing eye of the clock.

Just now she was standing at the side window of the nursery looking away across the roofs. The fat old gentleman at the gray-haired house was sponging off the rubber-plant, and waving the long green leaves at her in greeting. Gwendolyn feigned not to see. Her lips were firmly set. A scarlet spot of determination burned round either dimple. Her gray eyes smouldered darkly—with a purpose that was unswerving.

"I'm just going down there!" she said aloud.

Rustle! Rustle! Rustle!

It was Miss Royle, entering. Though Saturday was yet two days away, the governess was preparing to go out for the afternoon, and was busily engaged in drawing on her gloves, her glance alternating between her task and the time-piece on the school-room mantel.

"Gwendolyn dear," said she, "you can have such a *lovely* long pretend-game between now and supper, *can't* you?"

Gwendolyn moved her head up and down in slow assent. Doing so, she rubbed the tip of her nose against the smooth glass. The glass was cool. She liked the feel of it.

"You can travel!" enthused Miss Royle. "And *where* do you think you'll go?"

The gray eyes were searching the tiers of windows in a distant granite pile. "Oh, Asia, I guess," answered Gwendolyn, indifferently. (She had lately reviewed the latter part of her geography.)

"Asia? Fine! And how will you travel, darling? In your sweet car?"

A pause. Miss Royle was habitually honeyed in speech and full of suggestions when she was setting out thus. She deceived no one. Yet—it was just as well to humor her.

"Oh, I'll ride a musk-ox. Or"—picking at random from the fauna of the world—"or a llama, or a'—a' el'phunt." She rubbed her nose so hard against the glass that it gave out a squeaking sound.

"Then off you go!" and, *Rustle! Rustle! Rustle!*

Gwendolyn whirled. This was the moment, if ever, to make her wish known —to assert her will. With a running patter of slippers, she cut off Miss Royle's progress.

"That tall building 'way, 'way down on the sky," she panted.

"Yes, dear?"—with a simper.

"Is *that* where my father is?"

The smirk went. Miss Royle stared down. "Er—why?" she asked.

"'Cause"—the other's look was met squarely—"'cause I'm going down there to see him."

"Ah!" breathed the governess.

"I'm going to-day," went on Gwendolyn, passionately. "I want to!" Her lips trembled. "There's something—"

"Something you want to tell him, dear?"—purringly.

Confusion followed boldness. Gwendolyn dropped her chin, and made reply with an inarticulate murmur.

"Hm!" coughed Miss Royle. (Her *hms* invariably prepared the way for important pronouncements.)

Gwendolyn waited—for all the familiar arguments: I can't let you go until you're sent for, dear; Your papa doesn't want to be bothered; and, This is probably his busy day.

Instead, "Has anyone ever told you about that street, Gwennie?"

"No,"—still with lowered glance.

"Well, I wouldn't go down into it if *I* were you." The tone was full of hidden meaning.

There was a moment's pause. Then, "Why *not?*" asked Gwendolyn, back against the door. The question was put as a challenge. She did not expect an answer.

An answer came, however. "Well, I'll tell you: The street is full of—bears."

Gwendolyn caught her hands together in a nervous grasp. All her life she had heard about bears—and never any good of them. According to Miss Royle and Jane, these dread animals—who existed in all colors, and in nearly all climes—made it their special office to eat up little girls who disobeyed. She knew where several of the beasts were harbored—in cages at the Zoo, from where they sallied at the summons of outraged nurses and governesses.

But as to their being Down-Town—!

She lifted a face tense with earnestness "Is it *true?*" she asked hoarsely.

"My dear," said Miss Royle, gently reproving, "ask *any*body."

Gwendolyn reflected. Thomas was freely given to exaggeration. Jane, at times, resorted to bald falsehood. But Gwendolyn had never found reason to doubt Miss Royle.

She moved aside.

The governess turned to the school-room mirror to take a peep at her poke, and slung the chain of her hand-bag across her arm. Then, "I'll be home early," she said pleasantly. And went out by the door leading into the nursery.

Bears!

Gwendolyn stood bewildered. Oh, *why* were the Zoo bears in her father's street? Did it mean that he was in danger?

The thought sent her toward the nursery door. As she went she glanced back over a shoulder uneasily.

Close to the door she paused. Miss Royle was not yet gone, for there was a faint rustling in the next room. And Gwendolyn could hear the quick *shoo-ish, shoo-ish, shoo-ish* of her whispering, like the low purl of Johnnie Blake's trout-stream.

Presently, silence.

Gwendolyn went in.

She found Jane standing in the center of the room, mouth puckered soberly, reddish eyes winking with disquiet, apprehension in the very set of her heavy shoulders.

The sight halted Gwendolyn, and filled her with misgivings. Had *Jane* just heard?

When it came time to prepare for the afternoon motor-ride, Gwendolyn tested the matter—yet without repeating Miss Royle's dire statement.

"Let's go past where my fath-er's office is to-day," she proposed. And tried to smile.

Jane was tucking a small hand through a coat-sleeve. "Well, dearie," she answered, with a sigh and a shake of her red head, "you couldn't hire *me* to go into that street. And I wouldn't like to see *you* go."

Gwendolyn paled. "Bears?" she asked. "*Truly?*"

Jane made big eyes. Then turning the slender little figure carefully about, "Gwendolyn, lovie, *Jane* thinks you'd better give the idear up."

So it was true! Jane—who was happiest when standing in opposition to others; who was certain to differ if a difference was possible—Jane had borne it out!

Moreover, she was frightened! For Gwendolyn was leaning against the nurse. And she could feel her shaking!

Oh, how one terrible thing followed another!

Gwendolyn felt utterly cast down. And the ride in the swift-flying car only increased her dejection. For she did not even have the entertainment afforded by Thomas's enlivening company. He stayed beside the chauffeur —as he had, indeed, ever since the memorable feast of peanuts—and avoided turning his haughty black head. Jane was morose. Now and then, for no apparent reason, she sniffled.

Gwendolyn's mind was occupied by a terrifying series of pictures that Miss Royle's declaration called up. The central figure of each picture was her father, his safety threatened. Arrived home, she resolved upon still another course of action. She was forced to give up visiting her father at his office. But she would steal down to the grown-up part of the house—at a time *other* than the dinner-hour—that very night!

Evening fell, and she was not asked to appear in the great dining-room. That strengthened her determination. However, to give a hint of it would be folly. So, while Miss Royle picked at a chop and tittered over copious draughts of tea, and Thomas chattered unrebuked, she ate her supper in silence.

Ordinarily she rebelled at being undressed. She was not sleepy. Or she wanted to watch the Drive. Or she did not believe it was seven—there was something wrong with the clock. But supper over, and seven o'clock on the strike, she went willingly to bed.

When Gwendolyn was under the covers, and all the shades were down, Jane stepped into the school-room, leaving the door slightly ajar. She snapped on the lights above the school-room table. Then Gwendolyn heard the crackling of a news-paper.

She lay thinking. Why had she not been asked to the great dining-room? At seven her father—if all were well—should be sitting down to his dinner. But was he ill to-night? or hurt?

A half-hour dragged past. Jane left her paper and tiptoed into the nursery. Gwendolyn did not speak or move. When the nurse approached the bed and looked down, Gwendolyn shut her eyes.

Jane tiptoed out, closing the door behind her. A moment later Gwendolyn heard another door open and shut, then the rumble of a man's deep voice, and the shriller tones of a woman.

The chorus of indistinct voices made Gwendolyn sleepy. She found her eyelids drooping in spite of herself. That would never do! To keep herself awake, she got up cautiously, put on her slippers and dressing-gown, stole to the front window, climbed upon the long seat, and drew aside the shade —softly.

The night was moonless. Clouds hid the stars. The street lamps disclosed the crescent of the Drive only dimly. Beyond the Drive the river stretched like a smooth wide ribbon of black satin. It undulated gently. Upon the dark water of the farther edge a procession of lights laid a fringe of gold.

There were other lights—where, beyond the precipice, stood the forest houses; where moored boats rocked at a landing-place up-stream; and on boats that were plying past. A few lights made star-spots on the cliff-side.

But most brilliant of all were those forming the monster letters of words. These words Gwendolyn did not pronounce. For Miss Royle, whenever she chanced to look out and see them, said "Shameful!" or "What a disgrace!" or "Abominable!" And Gwendolyn guessed that the words were wicked.

As she knelt, peering out, sounds from city and river came up to her. There was the distant roll of street-cars, the warning; *honk! honk!* of an automobile, the scream of a tug; and lesser sounds—feet upon the sidewalk under the window, low laughter from the dim, tree-shaded walk.

She wondered about her father.

Suddenly there rose to her window a long-drawn cry. She recognized it—the high-keyed, monotonous cry of a man who often hurried past with a bundle of newspapers under his arm. Now it startled her. It filled her with foreboding.

"Uxtra! Uxtra! A-a-all about the lubble-lubble-lubble in ump Street!"

Street! *What* street? Gwendolyn strained her ears to catch the words. What if it were the street where her fath—

"Uxtra! Uxtra!" cried the voice again. It was nearer, yet the words were no clearer. "A-a-all about the lubble-lubble-lubble in ump Street!"

He passed. His cry died in the distance. Gwendolyn let the window-shade go back into place very gently. To prepare properly for her trip downstairs meant running the risk of discovery. She tiptoed noiselessly to the school-room door. There she listened. Thomas's deep voice was still rumbling on. Punctuating it regularly was a sniffle. And the key-hole showed a spot of glinting red—Jane's hair.

Gwendolyn left the school-room door for the one opening on the hall.

In the hall were shaded lights. Light streamed up the bronze shaft. Gwendolyn put her face against the scrolls and peered down. The cage was far below. And all was still.

The stairs wound their carpeted length before her. She slipped from one step to another warily, one hand on the polished banisters to steady herself, the other carrying her slippers. At the next floor she stopped before crossing the hall—to peer back over a shoulder, to peer ahead down the second flight.

Outside the high carved door of the library she stopped and put on the slippers. And she could not forbear wishing that she knew which was really her best foot, so that she might put it forward. But there was no time for conjectures. She bore down with both hands on the huge knob, and pressed her light weight against the panels. The heavy door swung open. She stole in.

The library had three windows that looked upon the side street. These windows were all set together, the middle one being built out farther than the other two, so as to form an embrasure. Over against these windows, in the shallow bow they formed, was a desk, of dark wood, and glass-topped. It was scattered with papers and books. Before it sat her father.

The moment her eyes fell upon him she realized that she had not come any too soon. For his shoulders were bent as from a great weight. His head was bowed. His face was covered by his hands.

She went forward swiftly. When she was between the desk and the windows she stopped, but did not speak. She kept her gray eyes on those shielding hands.

Presently he sighed, straightened on his chair, and looked at her.

For one instant Gwendolyn did not move—though her heart beat so wildly that it stirred the lace ruffles of her dressing-gown. Then, remembering dancing instructions, she curtsied.

A smile softened the stern lines of her father's mouth. It traveled up his cheeks in little ripples, and half shut his tired eyes. He put out a hand.

"Why, hello, daughter," he said wearily, but fondly.

She felt an almost uncontrollable desire to throw out her arms to him, to clasp his neck, to cry, "Oh, daddy! daddy! I don't want them to hurt you!" But she conquered it, her underlip in her teeth, and put a small hand in his outstretched one gravely.

"I—I heard the man calling," she began timidly. "And I—I thought maybe the bears down in your street—"

"Ah, the bears!" He gave a bitter laugh.

So Miss Royle had told the truth! The hand in his tightened its hold. "Have the bears ever frightened *you?*" she asked, her voice trembling.

He did not answer at once, but put his head on one side and looked at her— for a full half-minute. Then he nodded. "Yes," he said; "yes, dear,—once or twice."

She had planned to spy out at least a strap of the harness he wore; to examine closely what sort of candles, if any, he burned in the seclusion of the library. Now she forgot to do either; could not have seen if she had tried. For her eyes were swimming, blinding her.

She swayed nearer him. "If—if you'd take Thomas along on your car," she suggested chokingly. "He hunted el'phunts once, and—and *I* don't need him."

Her father rose. He was not looking at her—but away, beyond the bowed windows, though the shades of these were drawn, the hangings were in place. And, "No!" he said hoarsely; "not yet! I'm not through fighting them *yet!*"

"Daddy!" Fear for him wrung the cry from her.

His eyes fell to her upturned face. And as if he saw the terror there, he knelt, suddenly all concern. "Who told you about the bears, Gwendolyn?"— with a note of displeasure.

"Miss Royle."

"That was wrong—she shouldn't have done it. There are things a little girl can't understand." His eyes were on a level with her brimming ones.

The next moment—"Gwendolyn! *Gwen*dolyn! Oh, where's that child!" The voice was Jane's. She was pounding her way down the stairs.

Before Gwendolyn could put a finger to his lips to plead for silence, "Here, Jane," he called, and stood up once more.

Jane came in, puffing with her haste. "Oh, thank you, sir," she cried. "It give me *such* a turn, her stealin' off like that! Madam doesn't like her to be up late, as she well knows. And I'll be blamed for this, sir, though I take pains to follow out Madam's orders exact," She seized Gwendolyn.

Gwendolyn, eyes dry now, and defiant, pulled back with all the strength of her slender arm. "Oh, fath-er!" she plead. "Oh, *please*, I don't want to go!"

"Why! Why! Why!" It was reproval; but tender reproval, mixed with mild amazement.

"Oh, I want to tell you something," cried Gwendolyn. "Let me stay just a *minute*."

"That's just the way she acts, sir, whenever it's bed-time," mourned Jane.

He leaned to lift Gwendolyn's chin gently. "Father thinks she'd better go now," he said quietly. "And she's not to worry her blessed baby head any more." Then he kissed her.

The kiss, the knowledge that strife was futile, the sadness of parting—these brought the great sobs. She went without resisting, but stumbling a little; the back of one hand was laid against her streaming eyes.

Half a flight up the stairs, Jane turned her right about at a bend. Then she dropped the hand to look over the banisters. And through a blur of tears saw her father watching after her, his shoulders against the library door.

He threw a kiss.

Then another bend of the staircase hid his upturned face.

CHAPTER VI

Gwendolyn was lying on her back in the middle of the nursery floor. The skein of her flaxen hair streamed about her shoulders in tangles. Her head being unpillowed, her face was pink—and pink, too, with wrath. Her blue-and-white frock was crumpled. She was kicking the rug with both heels.

It was noon. And Miss Royle was having her dinner. Her face, usually so pale, was dark with anger—held well in check. Her expression was that of one who had recently suffered a scare, and her faded eyes shifted here and there uneasily. Thomas, too, looked apprehensive as he moved between table and tray. Jane was just gone, showing, as she disappeared, lips nervously pursed, and a red, roving glance that betokened worry.

Gwendolyn, watching out from under the arm that rested across her forehead, realized how her last night's breach of authority had impressed each one of them. And secretly rejoicing at her triumph, she kept up a brisk tattoo.

Miss Royle ignored her. "I'll take a little more chocolate, Thomas," she said, with a fair semblance of calm. But cup and saucer rattled in her hand.

Thomas, too, feigned indifference to the rat! tat! tat! of heels. He bent above the table attentively. And to Gwendolyn was wafted down a sweet aroma.

"Thank you," said Miss Royle. "And cake, *too?* Splendid! How did you manage it?" A knife-edge cut against china. She helped herself generously.

Gwendolyn fell silent to listen.

"Well, I haven't Mr. Potter to thank," said Thomas, warmly; "only my own forethoughtedness, as you might say. The first time I ever set eyes on it I seen it was the kind that'd keep, so—"

From under the shielding arm Gwendolyn blinked with indignation. *Her birthday cake!*

"Say, Miss Royle," chuckled Thomas, replenishing the chocolate cup, "that was a' *awful* whack you give Miss J—last night."

At once Gwendolyn forgot the wrong put upon her in the matter of the cake—in astonishment at this new turn of affairs. Evidently Miss Royle and Thomas were leagued against Jane!

The governess nodded importantly, "She *was* only a cook before she came here," she declared contemptuously. "Down at the Employment Agency, where Madam got her, they said so. The common, two-faced thing!" This last was said with much vindictiveness. Following it, she proffered Thomas the cake-plate.

"Thanks," said he; "I don't mind if I do have a slice."

Now, of a sudden, wrath and resentment possessed Gwendolyn, sweeping her like a wave—at seeing her cake portioned out; at having her kicking ignored; at hearing these two openly abuse Jane.

"I want some strawberries," she stormed, pounding the rug full force. "And an egg. I *won't* eat dry bread!" Bang! Bang! Bang!

Miss Royle half-turned. "Did you ask to go down to the library?" she inquired. She seemed totally undisturbed; yet her eyes glittered.

"Did she ask?" snorted Thomas. "She's gettin' very forward, she is."

"No, you knew better," went on Miss Royle. "You *knew* I wouldn't permit you to bother your father when he didn't want you—"

"He *did* want me!"—choking with a sob.

"Think," resumed the governess, inflecting her tones eloquently, "of the fortune he spends on your dresses, and your pony, and your beautiful car! And he hires all of us"—she swept a gesture—"to wait on you, you naughty girl, and try to make a little lady out of you—"

"I hate ladies!" cried Gwendolyn, rapping her heels by way of emphasis.

"Tale-bearing is *vulgar*," asserted Miss Royle.

"Next year I'm going to *day*-school like Johnnie *Blake!*"

"Oh, hush your nonsense!" commanded Thomas, irritably.

Miss Royle glanced up at him. "That will do," she snapped.

He bridled up. "What the little imp needs is a good paddlin'," he declared.

"Well, *you* have nothing to do with the disciplining of the child. That is *my* business."

"It's what she needs, all the same. The very idear of her bawlin' all the mornin' at the top of her lungs—"

"I did *not* at the top of my lungs," contradicted Gwendolyn. "I cried with my mouth."

"—So's the whole house can hear," continued Thomas; "and beatin' about the floor. It's clear shameful, *I* say, and enough to give a sensitive person the nerves. As I remarked to Jane only—-"

"You remark too many things to Jane," interposed the governess, curtly.

Now he sobered. "I *hope* you ain't displeased with me," he ventured.

"*Ain't* displeased?" repeated Miss Royle, more than ever fretful. "Oh, Thomas, *do* stop murdering the King's English!"

At that Gwendolyn sat up, shook back her hair, and raised a startled face to the row of toys in the glass-fronted case. Murdering the King's English! Had he *dared* to harm her soldier with the scarlet coat?

"I was urgin' your betterin', too, Miss Royle," reminded Thomas, gently. "I says to Jane, I says—"

The soldier was in his place, safe. Relieved, Gwendolyn straightened out once more on her back.

"—'The whole lot of us ought to be paid higher wages than we're gettin' for it's a real trial to have to be under the same roof with such a provokin'—'"

Miss Royle interrupted by vigorously bobbing her head. "Oh, that I have to make my living in this way!" she exclaimed, voice deep with mournfulness. "I'd rather wash dishes! I'd rather scrub floors! I'd rather *star-r-ve!*"

Something in the vehemence, or in the cadence, of Miss Royle's declaration again gave Gwendolyn that sense of triumph. With a sudden curling up of her small nose, she giggled.

Miss Royle whirled with a rustle of silk skirts. "Gwendolyn," she said threateningly, "if you're going to act like that, I shall know there's something the matter with you, and I shall certainly call a doctor."

Gwendolyn lay very still. As Thomas glanced down at her, smirking exultantly, her smile went, and the pink of wrath once more surged into her face.

"And the doctor'll give nasty medicine," declared Thomas, "or maybe he'll cut out your appendix!"

"Potter won't let him."

"Potter! Huh!—He'll cut out your appendix, and charge your papa a thousand dollars. Oh, you bet, them that's naughty always pays the piper."

Gwendolyn got to her feet. "I *won't* pay the piper," she retorted. "I'm going to give all my money to the hand-organ man—*all* of it. I like *him*," tauntingly. "But I hate—you."

"*We* hate a sneak," observed Miss Royle, blandly.

The little figure went rigid. "And I hate *you*," she cried shrilly. Then buried her face in her hands.

"*Gwen-do-lyn'!*" It was a solemn and horrified warning.

Gwendolyn turned and walked slowly toward the window-seat. Her breast was heaving.

"Come back and sit in this chair," bade the governess.

Gwendolyn paused, but did not turn.

"Shall I fetch you?"

"Can't I even look out of the window?" burst forth Gwendolyn. "Oh, you— you—you—" (she yearned to say Snake-in-the—grass!—yet dared not) "you mean! *mean!*" Her voice rose to a scream.

Miss Royle stood up. "I see that you want to go to bed," she declared.

The torrent of Gwendolyn's anger and resentment surged and broke bounds. She pivoted, arms tossing, face aflame. There were those wicked words across the river that each night burned themselves upon the dark. She had never pronounced them aloud before; but—

"Starch!" she shrilled, stamping a foot, "Villa sites! Borax! *Shirts!*"

Miss Royle gave Thomas a worried stare. He, in turn, fixed her with a look of alarm. So much Gwendolyn saw before she flung herself down again, sobbing aloud, but tearlessly, her cheek upon the rug.

She heard Miss Royle rustle toward the school-room; heard Thomas close the door leading into the hall. There were times—the nursery had seen a few—when the trio found it well to let her severely alone.

Now only a hoarse lamenting broke the quiet.

It was an hour later when some one tapped on the school-room door—Miss French, doubtless, since it was her allotted time. The lamentations swelled then—and grew fainter only when the last foot-fall died away on the stairs. Then Gwendolyn slept.

Awakening, she lay and watched out through the upper panes of the front window. Across the square of serene blue framed by curtains and casing, small clouds were drifting—clouds dazzlingly white. She pretended the clouds were fat, snowy sheep that were passing one by one.

Thus had snowy flocks crossed above the trout-stream. Oh? where was that stream? the glade through which it flowed? the shingled cottage among the trees?

With all her heart Gwendolyn wished she were a butterfly.

Suddenly she sat up. She had found her way alone to the library. Why not put on hat and coat *and go to Johnnie Blake's?*

She was at the door of the wardrobe before she remembered the kidnapers, and realized that she dared not walk out alone. But Potter liked the country. Besides, he knew the way. She decided to ask him to go with her—old and stooped though he was. Perhaps she would also take the pretty nurse-maid at the corner. And those who were left behind—Miss Royle and Thomas and Jane—would all be sorry when she was gone.

But let them fret! Let them weep, and wish her back! She—

That moment she caught sight of the photographs on the writing-desk. She stood still to look at them. As she looked, both pictured faces gradually dimmed. For tears had come at last—at the thought of leaving father and mother—quiet tears that flowed in erratic little S's between gray eyes and trembling mouth.

How could she forsake *them?*

"Gwendolyn," she half-whispered, "s'pose we just pu-play the Johnnie Blake Pretend ... Oh, very well,"—this last with all of Miss Royle's precise intonation.

The heavy brocade hangings were the forest trees. The piano was the mountain, richly inlaid. The table was the cottage, and she rolled it nearer the dull rose timber at the side window. The rug was the grassy, flowery glade; its border, the stream that threaded the glade. Beyond the stream twisted an unpaved and carefully polished road.

The first part of this particular Pretend was the drive to the village—carved and enameled, and paneled with woven cane. A hassock did duty for a runabout that had no top to shut out the sun-light, no windows to bar the fragrant air. In front of the hassock, a pillow did duty as a stout dappled pony.

Her father drove. And she sat beside him, holding on to the iron bar of the runabout seat with one hand, to a corner of his coat with the other; for not only were the turns sharp but the country road was uneven. The sun was just rising above the forest, and it warmed her little back. The fresh breeze caressed her cheeks into crimson, and swirled her hair about the down-sloping rim of her wreath-encircled hat. That breeze brought with it the perfume of opening flowers, the fragrance exhaled by the trees along the way, the essence of the damp ground stirred by hoof and wheel. Gwendolyn breathed through nostrils swelled to their widest.

Following the drive to the village came the trip up the stream to trout-pools. Gwendolyn's father led the way with basket and reel. She trotted at his heels. And beside Gwendolyn trotted Johnnie Blake.

The piano-seat was Johnnie. His eyes were blue, and full of laughter. His small nose was as freckled as Jane's. His brown hair disposed itself in several rough heaps, as if it had been winnowed by a tiny whirlwind.

"Good-morning," said Gwendolyn, curtseying.

"Hello!" returned Johnnie—while Gwendolyn smiled at herself in the pier-glass. Johnnie carried a long willow fishing-pole cut from the stream-side. Reel he had none, nor basket; and he did not own a belted outing-suit of hunter's-green, and high buckled boots. He wore a plaid gingham waist, starched so stiff that its round collar stood up and tickled his ears. His hat was of straw, and somewhat ragged. His brown jeans overalls, riveted and suspendered, reached to bare ankles fully as brown. The overalls were provided with three pockets. Bulging one was his round tin drinking-cup which was full of worms.

"Are there p'liceman in these woods?" inquired Gwendolyn.

"Nope," said Johnnie.

"Are there bears?"

"Nope."

"Are there doctors?"

"Nope. But there's snakes—some."

"Oh, I'm not afraid of snakes. I've got one at home. It's long and black, and it's got a wooden tongue."

"'Fraid to go barefoot?"

"Oh, I wish I could!"

Here she glanced over a shoulder toward the school-room; then toward the hall. Did she dare?

"Well, you're little yet," explained Johnnie. "But just you wait till you grow up."

"Are—are *you* grown-up?"—a trifle doubtfully.

"Of *course*, I'm grown up! Why, I'm *seven*." Whereat she strode up and down, hands on hips, in feeble imitation of Johnnie.

But here the inclination for further make-believe died utterly—at a point where, usually, Johnnie threw back his head with a triumphant laugh, gave a squirrel-like leap into the air (from the top of the nursery table), caught the lower branch of a tall, slim tree (the chandelier), and swung himself to and fro with joyous abandon. For Gwendolyn suddenly remembered the cruel truth borne out by the ink-line on the pier-glass. And instead of climbing upon the table, she went to stand in front of her writing-desk.

"I was seven my last birthday," she murmured, looking up at the rose-embossed calendar.

Seven, and grown-up—and yet everything was just the same!

She went to the front window and knelt on the cushioned seat. Across the river red smoke was pouring up from those chimneys on the water's edge that were assuredly a mile high. Red smoke meant that evening was approaching. Jane would enter soon. With two in the nursery, the advantage was for her who did not have to make the overtures of peace. She turned her back to the room.

Jane came. She drew the heavy curtains at the side window and busied herself in the vicinity of the bed, moving about quietly, saying not a word. Presently she went out.

Gwendolyn faced round. The bed was arranged for the night. At its head, on the small table, was a glass of milk, a sandwich, a cup of broth, a plate of cooked fruit.

The western sky faded—to gray, to deep blue, to jade. The river flowed jade beneath. Along it the lights sprang up. Then came the stars.

Gwendolyn worked at the buttons of her slippers. The tears were falling again; but not tears of anger or resentment—only of loneliness, of yearning.

The little white-and-blue frock fastened down the front. She undid it, weeping softly the while, found her night-dress, put it on and climbed into bed.

The food was close at hand. She did not touch it. She was not hungry, only worn with her day-long combat. She lay back among the pillows. And as she looked up at the stars, each sent out gay little flashes of light to every side.

"Oh, moth-er!" she mourned. "Everybody hates me! Everybody hates me!"

Then came a comforting thought: She would play the Dearest Pretend!

It was easy to make believe that a girlish figure was seated in the dark beside the bed; that a tender face was bending down, a gentle hand touching the troubled forehead, stroking the tangled hair.

"Oh, I want you all the time, moth-er!... And I want *you*, my precious baby.... How much do you love me, moth-er?... Love you?—oh, big as the sky!... Dear moth-er, may I eat at the grown-up table?... All the time, sweetheart.... Goody! And we'll just let Miss Royle eat with Jane and—"

She caught a stealthy *rustle! rustle! rustle!* from the direction of the hall. She spoke more low then, but continued to chatter, her pretend-conversation, loving, confidential, and consoling.

Finally, "Moth-er," she plead, "will you please sing?"

She sang. Her voice was husky from crying. More than once it quavered and broke. But the song was one she had heard in the long, raftered living-room at Johnnie Blake's. And it soothed.

> "Oh, it is not while beauty and youth are thine o-o-own,
> And thy cheek is unstained by a tear,
> That the fervor and faith of a soul can be kno-o-own—"

It grew faint. It ended—in a long sigh. Then one small hand in the gentle make-believe grasp of another, she slept.

CHAPTER VII

Miss Royle looked sober as she sipped her orange-juice. And she cut off the top of her breakfast egg as noiselessly as possible. Her directions to Thomas, she half-whispered, or merely signaled them by a wave of her coffee-spoon. Now and then she glanced across the room to the white-and-gold bed. Then she beamed fondly.

As for Thomas, he fairly stole from tray to table, from table to tray, his face all concern. Occasionally, if his glance followed Miss Royle's, he smiled—a broad, sympathetic smile.

And Jane was subdued and solicitous. She sat beside the bed, holding a small hand—which from time to time she patted encouragingly.

After the storm, calm. The more tempestuous the storm, the more perfect the calm. This was the rule of the nursery. Gwendolyn, lying among the pillows, wished she could always feel weak and listless. It made everyone so kind.

"Thomas," said Miss Royle, as she folded her napkin and rustled to her feet, "you may call up the Riding School and say that Miss Gwendolyn will not ride to-day."

"Yes, ma'am."

"And, Jane, you may go out for the morning. I shall stay here."

"Thanks," acknowledged Jane, in a tone quite unusual for her. She did not rise, however, but waited, striving to catch Thomas's eye.

"And, Thomas," went on the governess, "when would *you* like an hour?"

Thomas advanced with a bow of appreciation. "If it's all the same to you, Miss Royle," said he, "I'll have a bit of an airin' directly after supper this evenin'."

Jane glared.

"Very well." Miss Royle rustled toward the school-room, taking a survey of herself in the pier-glass as she went. "Jane," she added, "you will be free to go in half an hour." She threw Gwendolyn a loud kiss.

Thomas was directing his attention to the clearing of the breakfast-table. The moment the door closed behind the governess, Jane shot up from her chair and advanced upon him.

"You ain't treatin' me fair," she charged, speaking low, but breathing fast. "You ain't takin' your hours off duty along with me no more. You're givin' me the cold shoulder."

At that, Gwendolyn turned her head to look. Of late, she had heard not a few times of Thomas's cold shoulder—this in heated encounters between him and Jane. She wondered which of his shoulders was the cold one.

Thomas lifted his upper lip in a sneer. "Indeed!" he replied. "I'm not treatin' you fair? Well," (with meaning) "I didn't think you was botherin' your head about anybody—except a certain policeman."

Back jerked Jane's chin. "Can't I have a gentleman friend?" she demanded defensively.

"Ha! ha! Gentleman friend!" Then, addressing no one in particular, "My! but don't a uniform take a woman's eye!"

"Why, Thomas!" It was a sorrowful protest. "You misjudge, you really *do*."

So far there was no fresh element in the misunderstanding. Thus the two argued time and again. Gwendolyn almost knew their quarrel by heart.

But now Thomas came round upon Jane with a snarl. "You're not foolin' me," he declared. "Don't you think I know that policeman's heels over head?" He shook his crumb-knife at her. "*Heels over head!*" Then seizing the tray and swinging it up, he stalked out.

Jane fell to pacing the floor. Her reddish eyes roved angrily.

Heels over head! Gwendolyn, pondering, now watched the nurse, now looked across to where, on its shelf, was poised the toy somersault man. If one of the uniformed men she dreaded was heels over head—

"But, Jane."

"Well? Well?"

"I saw the p'liceman walking on his feet *yesterday*."

"Hush your silly talk!"

Gwendolyn hushed, her gray eyes wistful, her mouth drooping. The morning had been so peaceful. Now Jane had spoken the first rough word.

Peace returned with Miss Royle, who came in with the morning paper, dismissed Jane, and settled down in the upholstered chair, silver-rimmed spectacles on nose.

The brocade hangings of the front window were only partly drawn. Between them, Gwendolyn made out more of those fat sheep straying down the azure field of the sky. She lay very still and counted them; and, counting, slept, but restlessly, with eyes only half-shut and nervous starts.

Awakening at noon the listlessness was gone, and she felt stronger. Her eyes were bright, too. There was a faint color in cheeks and lips.

"Miss Royle!"

"Yes, darling?" The governess leaned forward attentively.

"I can understand why you call Thomas a footman. It's 'cause he runs around so much on his feet—"

"You're better," said Miss Royle. She turned her paper inside out.

"But one day you said he was all ears, and—"

"Gwendolyn!" Miss Royle stared down over her glasses. "Never repeat what you hear me say, love. It's tattling, and tattling is ill-bred. Now, what can I give you?"

Gwendolyn wanted a drink of water.

When Thomas appeared with the dinner-tray, he gave an impressive wag of the head. "*What* do you think I've got for you?" he asked—while Miss

Royle propped Gwendolyn to a sitting position.

Gwendolyn did not try to guess. She was not interested. She had no appetite.

Thomas brought forward a silver dish. "It's a bird!" he announced, and lifted the cover.

Gwendolyn looked.

It was a small bird, richly browned. A tiny sprig of parsley garnished it on either side. A ribbon of bacon lay in crisp flutings across it. Its short round legs were up-thrust. On the end of each was a paper frill.

"*Don't* it look delicious!" said Thomas warmly. "Don't it tempt!"

But Gwendolyn regarded it without enthusiasm. "What kind of a bird is it?" she asked.

Thomas displayed a second dish—Bermuda potatoes the size of her own small fist. "Who knows?" said he. "It might be a robin, it might be a plover, it might be a quail."

"It might be a—a talking-bird," said Gwendolyn. She poked the bird with a fork.

"Not likely," declared Thomas.

Gwendolyn turned away.

"Ain't it to your likin'?" asked Thomas, surprised. He did not take the plate at once, in his usual fashion.

"I—I don't want anything," she declared.

"Oh, but maybe you'd fancy an egg."

Gwendolyn took a glass of water.

"It's just as well," said Miss Royle. When she resigned her place presently, she talked to Jane in undertones,—so that Gwendolyn could hear only disconnectedly: "...Think it would be the safest thing ... she gets any worse.... Never do, Jane ... find out by themselves.... She won't be home till late to-night ... some grand affair. But he ... though of course I'm sorry to have to."

The moment Miss Royle was well away, Jane had a plan. "*I* think you're gittin' on so fine that you can hop up and dress," she declared, noting how the gray eyes sparkled, and how pink were the round spots on Gwendolyn's cheeks.

Gwendolyn had nothing to say.

Jane ran to the wardrobe and took out a dress. It was a new one, of cream-white wool; and on a sleeve, as well as on the corners of the sailor collar and the tips of the broad tie, scarlet anchors were embroidered.

Gwendolyn smiled. But it was not the anchors that charmed forth the smile. It was a pocket, set like a shield on the blouse—an adorable patch-pocket!

"Oh!" she cried; "did They make me that pocket? Jane, how sweet!"

"One, two, three," said Jane, briskly, "and we'll have this on! Let's see by the clock how quick you can jump into it!"

The clock was a familiar method of inducing Gwendolyn to do hastily something she had not thought of doing at all. She shook her head.

"Why, it'd do you *good*, pettie,"—this coaxingly.

"It's too warm to dress," said Gwendolyn.

Jane flung the garment back into the wardrobe without troubling to hang it up, and banged the wardrobe door. But she did not again broach the subject of getting up. A hint of uneasiness betrayed itself in her manner. She took a chair by the bed.

Gwendolyn's whole face was gradually taking on a deep flush, for those flaming spots on her cheeks were spreading to throat and temples—to her very hair. She kept her hands in constant motion. Next, the small tongue began to babble uninterruptedly.

It was the overlively talking that made Jane certain that Gwendolyn was ill. She leaned to feel of the busy hands, the throbbing forehead. Then she hastily telephoned Thomas.

"Have we any more of that quietin' medicine?" she asked as he opened the door.

"It's all gone. Why?"

The two forgot their differences, and bent over Gwendolyn.

She smiled up, and nodded. "All the clouds in the sky are filled with wind," she declared; "like automobile tires. Toy-balloons are, I know. Once I put a pin in one, and the wind blew right out. I s'pose the clouds in the South hold the south wind, and the clouds in the North hold the north wind, and the clouds—"

"Jane," said Thomas, "we've got to have a doctor."

Gwendolyn heard. She saw Jane spring to the telephone. The next instant, with a piercing scream that sent her canary fluttering to the top of its cage, she flung herself sidewise.

"Jane! Oh, don't! Jane! He'll kill me! *Jane!*"

Jane fell back, and caught Gwendolyn in her arms. The little figure was all a-tremble, both small hands were beating the air in wild protest.

"Jane! Oh, I'll be good! I'll be good!" She hid her face against the nurse, shuddering.

"But you're sick, lovie. And a doctor would make you well. There! There! Listen to Jane, dearie."

Thomas laid an anxious hand on the yellow head. "The doctor won't hurt you," he declared. "He only gives bread-pills, anyhow."

"*No-o-o!*" She flung herself back upon the bed, catching at the pillows as if to hide beneath them, writhing pitifully, moaning, beseeching with terrified eyes.

Jane and Thomas stared helplessly at each other, their faces guilty and frightened.

"Dearie!" cried Jane; "hush and we won't—Oh, Thomas, I'm fairly distracted!—Pettie, we *won't* have the doctor."

Gradually Gwendolyn quieted. Then carefully, and by degrees, Jane approached the matter of medical aid in a new way.

"We'll just telephone," she declared, "We wont let any old doctor come here —not a *bit* of it. We'll ask him to send something. Is *that* all right. *Please*, darlin'."

Reluctantly, Gwendolyn yielded. "The medicine'll be awful nasty," she faltered.

To that Jane made no reply. Her every freckle was standing out clearly. Her reddish eyes bulged. She hunted a number in the telephone-directory with fumbling fingers. After which she held the receiver to her ear with a shaking hand. "Everything's goin' wrong," she mourned.

Huddled into a little ball, and still as a frightened bird, Gwendolyn listened to the message.

"Hello!... Hello! Is this the Doctor speakin'?... Oh, this is Miss Gwendolyn's nurse, sir.... *Yes* sir. Well, Miss Gwendolyn's a little nervous to-day, sir. Not sick enough to call you in, sir.... But I was goin' to ask if you couldn't send something soothin'. She's been cryin' like, that's all.... Yes, sir, and wakeful —"

"A little hysterical yesterday," prompted Thomas, in a low voice.

"A little hysterical yesterday," went on Jane. "...Yes, sir, by messenger.... I'll be *most* careful, sir.... Thank you, sir."

Jane and Thomas combined to make the remainder of the afternoon less dull. One by one the favorite toys came down from the second shelf. And a miniature circus took place on the rug beside the bed—a circus in which each toy played a part. Gwendolyn's fear was charmed away. She laughed, and drank copious draughts of water—delicious bubbling water that Thomas poured from tall bottles.

Jane had her own supper beside the white-and-gold bed—coffee and a sandwich only. Gwendolyn still had no appetite, but seemed almost her usual self once more. So much so that when she asked questions, Jane was cross, and counseled immediate sleep.

"But I'm not a bit sleepy," declared Gwendolyn. "It'll be moonlight after while, Jane. May I look out at the Down-Town roofs?"

"You may stop your botherin'," retorted Jane, "and make up your mind to go to sleep. You've give me a' awful day. Now try just forty winks."

"Why do you always say forty?" inquired Gwendolyn. "Couldn't I take forty-one?"

"*Hush!*"

After supper came the medicine—a dark liquid. Gwendolyn eyed it anxiously. Thomas was gone. Jane opened the bottle and measured a teaspoonful into a drinking-glass.

"Do I have to take it now?" asked Gwendolyn.

"To-morrow you'll wake up as good as new," asserted Jane. She touched her tongue with the spoon, then smacked her lips. "Why, dearie, it's—"

She was interrupted. From the direction of the side window there came a burst of instrumental music. With it, singing the words of a waltz from a popular opera, blended a thin, cracked voice.

Before Jane could put out a restraining hand, Gwendolyn bounced to her knees. "Oh, it's the old hand-organ man!" she cried. "It's the old hand-organ man! Oh, where's some money? I want to give him some money!"

Jane threw up both hands wildly. "Oh, did I ever have such luck!" she exclaimed. Then, between her teeth, and pressing Gwendolyn back upon the pillows, "You lay down or I'll shake you!"

"Oh, please let him stay just this time!" begged Gwendolyn; "I like him, Jane!"

"I'll stay him!" promised Jane, grimly. She marched to the side window, threw up the sash and leaned out. "Here, you!" she called down roughly. "You git!"

"Oh, Jane!" plead Gwendolyn.

The thin, cracked voice fell silent. The waltz slowed its tempo, then came to a gasping stop.

"How's a body to git a child asleep with that old wheeze of yours goin'?" demanded Jane. "We don't *want* you here. Move along!"

"He could play me to sleep," protested Gwendolyn.

A reply to Jane's order was shrilled up—something defiant.

"He'd only excite you, darlin'," declared Jane. She was on her knees at the window, and turned her head to speak. "I can't have that rumpus in the street with you so nervous."

Gwendolyn sighed.

"Take your medicine, dearie," went on Jane. She stayed where she was.

Promptly, Gwendolyn sat up and reached for the glass. To hold it, to shake it about and potter in the strange liquid with a spoon, would be some compensation for having to drink it.

"If that mean old creature didn't make faces!" grumbled Jane. She was leaning forward to look out.

"*How* did he make faces, Jane?" asked Gwendolyn. "Were they nice ones?" She lifted the glass to take a whiff of its contents. "I'd like to see him make faces."

She put the spoon into Jane's half-empty coffee-cup; then let the medicine run up the side of the glass until it was almost to her lips. She tasted it. It tasted good! She hesitated a second; then drained the glass.

The street was quiet. Jane rose to her feet and came over. "Did you do as I said?" she asked.

"Yes, Jane."

"Now, *did* you?" Jane picked up the glass, looked into it, then at Gwendolyn. "Honest?"

"Yes,—every sip."

"*Gwendolyn?*" Jane held her with doubting eyes. "I don't believe it!"

"But I *did!*"

Jane bent down to the cup, sniffed it, then smelled of the glass.

"Gwendolyn," she said solemnly, "I know you did *not* take your medicine. You poured it into this cup."

"But I *didn't!*"

"I *seen.*" Jane pointed an accusing finger.

"How *could* you?" demanded Gwendolyn. "You were looking at the brick house."

"I've got eyes in the back of my head. And I seen you *plain* when I was lookin' straight the other way."

"A-a-aw!" laughed Gwendolyn, skeptically.

"They're hid by my braids," went on Jane, "but they're there. And I seen you throw away that medicine, you bad girl!" Again she leaned to examine the coffee-cup.

"Miss Royle said you had two faces," admitted Gwendolyn. She stared hard at the coiled braids on the back of Jane's head. The braids were pinned close together. No pair of eyes was visible.

Jane straightened resolutely, seized the medicine-bottle and the spoon, poured out a second dose, and proffered it. "Come, now!" she said firmly. "You ain't a-goin' to git ahead of me with your cuteness. Take this, and go to sleep."

"Bu-but—"

That moment a shrill whistle sounded from the street.

"*There* now!" cried Jane, triumphantly. "The policeman's right here. I can call him up whenever I like."

Gwendolyn drank.

Jane tossed the spoon aside, corked the bottle and went back to the open window. "You go to sleep," she commanded.

Gwendolyn, lying flat, was murmuring to herself. "Oo-oo! How funny!" she said, "Oo-oo!"

"Now, don't let me hear another word out of you!" warned Jane.

Gwendolyn turned her head slowly from side to side. A great light of some kind was flaming against her eyes—a light shot through and through with black, whirling balls. Where did it come from?

It stayed. And grew. Her eyes widened with wonderment. A smile curved her lips.

Then suddenly she rose to a sitting posture, threw out both arms, and gave a little choking cry.

CHAPTER VIII

It was a cry of amazement. For suddenly—so suddenly that she did not have time to think how it had happened—she found herself *up and dressed,* and standing alone, gazing about her, *in the open air!*

But there were no high buildings on any side, no people passing to and fro, no motor-cars flashing by. And the grass underfoot was not the grass of a lawn, evenly cut and flowerless; it was tall, so that it brushed the hem of her dress, and blossom-dotted.

She looked up at the sky. It was not the sky of the City, distant, and marbled with streaks of smoke. It was close and clear; starless, too; and no moon hung upon it. Yet though it was night there was light everywhere—warm, glowing, roseate.

By that radiant glow she saw that she was in the midst of trees! Some were tall and slender and clean-barked; others were low and thick of trunk, but with the wide shapely spread of the great banyan in her geography; and, towering above the others, were the giants of that forest, unevenly branched, misshapen, aslant, and rugged with wart-like burls.

"Is—is this the Park?" she said aloud, still looking around. "Or—or the woods across the River?"

But there was no sign of a paved walk, such as traced patterns through the Park; nor of a chimney, to mark the whereabouts of a house. Behind her the ground sloped gently up to a wooded rise; in front of her it sloped as gently down to the edge of a narrow, noisy mountain stream.

"Why, I'm at Johnnie Blake's!" she cried—then glanced over a shoulder cautiously. If this were indeed the place she had longed to revisit, it would be advisable to keep as quiet as possible, lest someone should hear her, and straightway come to take her home.

Still watching backward apprehensively, she pushed through the grass to the edge of the stream.

The moment she reached it she knew that it was not the trout-stream along which she had wandered while her father fished. It was, in fact, not ordinary water at all, but something lighter, more sparkling with color, swifter, and louder. It effervesced, so that a creamy mist lay along its surface—this the smoke of bursting bubbles. It was like the bottled water she drank at her nursery meals!

Hands clasped, she leaned to stare down. "Isn't it *funny!*" she exclaimed half under her breath.

A voice answered her—from close at hand. It was a thin, cracked voice. "This is where They get their soda-water," it said.

She turned, and saw him.

He was a queer little old thick-set, dark-skinned gentleman, with grizzled whiskers, a ragged hat and baggy trousers. His eyes were round and black under his brows, which were square and long-haired, and not unlike a certain new hand-brush that Jane wielded of a morning across Gwendolyn's small finger-tips. Over one shoulder, by a strap, hung a dark box, half-hidden by a piece of old carpet. In one hand he held a huge, curved knife.

Though she could not remember ever having seen him at Johnnie Blake's; and though the curved knife was in pattern the true type of a kidnaper's weapon, and the look out of those round, dark eyes, as he strode toward her, was not at all friendly, she did not scamper away. She waited, her heart beating hard. When he halted, she curtsied.

"I've—I've always wondered about soda-water," she faltered, trying to smile. "But when I asked—"

"Um!" he grunted; then, with a sidewise jerk of the head, "Take a drink."

She lifted eager eyes. "All I *want* to?" she half-whispered.

He nodded. "Sip! Lap! Tipple!"

"Oo!" Fairly beaming with delight, she knelt down. For the first time in her life she could have all the soda-water she wanted!

First, she put the tip of one finger into the rushing sparkle, slowly, to lengthen out her joy. Next, with a little laugh, she sank her whole hand. Bubbles formed upon it,—all sizes of them—standing out like dewdrops upon leaves. The bubbles cooled. And tempted her thirst. With a deep breath, she bent forward until her red mouth touched the shimmering surface. Thus, lying prone, with arms spread wide, she drank deep of the flow.

When she straightened and sat back upon her heels, she made an astonishing discovery: The trees that studded the slope were not covered with leaves, like ordinary trees! Each branched to hold lights—myriads of lights! Some of these shone steadily; others burned with a hissing sound; others were silent enough, but rose and fell, jumped and flickered. It was these countless lights that illumed the forest like a pink sun.

She rose. There was wonder in the gray eyes. "Are these Christmas trees?" she said. "Where am I?"

"You've had your soda-water," he answered shortly. "You ought to know."

"Yes, I—I ought to know. But—I don't."

He grunted.

"I s'pose," she ventured timidly, "that nobody ever answers questions here, either."

He looked uncomfortable. "Yes," he retorted, "*every*body does."

"Then,"—advancing an eager step—"why don't *you*?"

He mopped his forehead. "Well—well—if I must, I must: This is where all the lights go when they're put out at night."

"Oh!" And now as she glanced from tree to tree she saw that what he had said was true. For the greater part of the lights were electric bulbs; while many were gas-jets, and a few kerosene-flames.

Still marveling, her look chanced to fall upon herself. And she found that she was not wearing a despised muslin frock! Her dress was gingham!—an adorable plaid with long sleeves, and a patch-pocket low down on the right side!

"You darling!" she exclaimed happily, and thrust a hand into the pocket. "I guess They made it!"

Next she looked down at her feet—and could scarcely believe! She had on no stockings! She did not even have on slippers. *She was barefoot!*

Then, still fearful that there was some mistake about it all, she put a hand to her head; and found her hair-bow gone! In its place, making a small floppy double knot, was a length of black shoe-string!

"Oh, goody!" she cried.

"Um!" grunted the little old gentleman. "And you can play in the water if you'd like to."

That needed no urging! She was face about on the instant.

From the standpoint of messing the soda-stream was ideal. It brawled around flat rocks, set at convenient jumping-distances from one another. (She leaped promptly to one of these and sopped her handkerchief.) It circled into sand-bottomed pools just shallow enough for wading; and from the pools, it spread out thinly to thread the grass, thus giving her an opportunity for squashing—a diverting pastime consisting in squirting equal parts of water and soil ticklishly through the toes. She hopped from rock to pool; she splashed from pool to long, wet, muddy grass.

It was the water-play that brought the realization of all her new good-fortune—the being out of doors and plainly clad; free from the espionage of a governess; away from the tyranny of a motor-car; barefoot; and—chief blessing of all!—*nurseless*.

Forgetting the little old gentleman, in a sudden excess of glee she seized a stick and bestrode it; seized another and belabored the quarters of a stout dappled pony; pranced, reared, kicked up her wet feet, shied wildly—

Then, both sticks cast aside, she began to dance; at first with deliberation, holding out the gingham dress at either side, and mincing through the steps taught by Monsieur Tellegen. But gradually she forsook rhythm and measure; capering ceased; the dance became fast and furious. Hallooing, she raced hither and thither among the trees, tossing her arms, darting down at the flowers and flinging them high, swishing her yellow hair from side to side, leaping exultantly toward the lights, pivoting—

Suddenly she found that she was dancing to music!—not the laboriously strummed notes of a piano, such as were beaten out by the firm-striding Miss Brown; not the clamorous, deafening, tuneless efforts of an orchestra. This was *real* music—inviting, inspiring, heavenly!

It was a hand-organ!

She halted, spell-bound. He was playing, turning the crank with a swift, steady motion, his ragged hat tipped to one side.

Now she understood the box hanging from its strap. She danced up to him, and held out a hand. "Why, you're the *hand-organ* man!" she panted breathlessly. "And you got here as quick as I did!"

He stopped playing, "I'm the hand-organ man when I'm in town," he corrected. "Here, in the Land of the Lights, I'm the Man-Who-Makes-Faces."

The Man-Who-Makes-Faces! She looked at him with new interest. "Why, of course you are," she acknowledged. "Sometimes you make 'em in town."

"Sometimes in town I make an ugly one," he retorted. Whereupon he shouldered the hand-organ, grasped the curved knife, and started away. As he walked, he called aloud to every side, like a huckster.

"Here's where you get your ears sharpened!" he sang. "*Ears* sharpened! *Eyes* sharpened! Edges taken off of tongues!"

She trotted beside him, head up, gray eyes wide, lips parted. He was ascending a gentle rise toward a low hill not far distant. As she drew away from the stream and the glade, she heard, from somewhere far behind, a shrill voice. It called a name—a name strangely familiar. She paid no heed.

At the summit of the little hill, under some trees, he paused, and waved the kidnaper knife in circles. "*Ears* to sharpen!" he shrilled again. "*Eyes* to sharpen! Edges taken off of tongues!"

She smiled up at him engagingly, noting how his gray hair hung over the back of his collar. She felt no fear of him whatever. "I think you're nice, Mr. Man-Who-Makes-Faces," she announced presently. "I'm so glad I can look straight at you. I didn't know you, 'cause your voice is different, and 'cause I'd never seen you before 'cept when I was looking *down* at you."

He had been ignoring her. But now, "Wasn't my fault that we didn't meet face to face," he retorted. Though his voice was still cross, his round, bright eyes were almost kind. "If you'll remember I often came under your window."

"And I threw you money," she answered, nodding brightly. "I wanted to come down and talk to you, oh, lots of times, only—"

At that, he relented altogether. And, reaching out, shook hands cordially. "Wouldn't you like," said he, "to have a look at my establishment?" He jerked a thumb over a shoulder. "Here's where I make faces."

In the City she had seen many wonderful shops, catching glimpses of some from the little window of her car, visiting others with Miss Royle or Jane. Among the former were those fascinating ones, usually low of ceiling and dark with coal-dust, where grimy men in leather aprons tried shoes on horses; and those horrifying places past which she always drove with closed eyes—places where, scraped white and head downward, hung little pigs, pitiful husks of what they once had been, flanked on either hand by long-necked turkeys with poor glazed eyes; and once she had seen a wonderful shop in which men were sawing out flat pieces of stone, and writing words on them with chisels.

But this shop of the Man-Who-Makes-Faces was the most interesting of all.

It occupied a square of hard-packed ground—a square as broad as the nursery. And curiously enough, like the nursery, it had, marking it off all the way around its outer edge, a border of flowers!

It was shaded by one huge tree.

"Lime-tree," explained the little old gentleman. "And the lights—"

"Don't tell me!" she cried. "I know! They're lime lights."

These made the shop exceedingly bright. Full in their glare, neatly disposed, were two short-legged tables, a squat stool, and a high, broad bill-board.

The Man-Who-Makes-Faces seated himself on the stool at one of the tables and began working industriously.

But Gwendolyn could only stand and stare about her, so amazed that she was dumb. For in front of the little old gentleman, and spread handily, were ears and eyes, noses and mouths, cheeks and chins and foreheads. And upon the bill-board, pendant, were toupees and side-burns and mustaches, puffs, transformations and goatees—and one coronet braid (a red one) glossy and thick and handsome!

The bill-board also held an assortment of tongues—long and scarlet. These, a score in all, were ranged in a shining row. And underneath them was a sign which bore this announcement:

Gwendolyn clapped her hands. "Oo! how *nice!*" she exclaimed, finding her voice again.

"Quite so," said the little old gentleman, shoving away a tray of chins and cheeks and reaching for a forehead. "Welcome, convenient, and satisfactory."

She saw her opportunity. "Please," she began, "I'd like to buy six." She counted on her fingers. "I'll have a French tongue, a German tongue, a Greek tongue, a Latin tongue, and—later, though, if you don't happen to have 'em on hand—a Spanish and an Italian." Then she heaved a sigh of relief. "I'm glad I saw these," she added. "They'll save me a lot of work. And they've helped me about a def'nition. I looked for 'lashing' in my big dictionary. And it said 'to whip.' But *I* couldn't see how anybody could whip anybody else with a *tongue*. Now, though—"

The Man-Who-Makes-Faces nodded. "Just wait till you see the King's English," he bragged.

"The King's English? Will I see him?"

"Likely to," he answered, selecting an eye. He had all his eyes about him in a circle, each looking as natural as life. There were blue eyes and brown eyes, hazel eyes and—

"Ah!" she exclaimed suddenly. "I remember! It was *you* who gave the Policeman a black eye!"

"One *fine* black eye," he answered, chuckling as he poked about in a pile of noses and selected a large-sized one. "Yes! Yes! And recently I made a lovely blue pair for a bad-tempered child who'd cried her own eyes out."

She assented. She had heard of just such a case. "Once I saw some eyes in a shop-window," she confided. "It was a shop where you could buy spectacles."

He wagged his beard proudly. "I made every *one* of 'em!" he boasted. "Oh, yes, indeed." And polished away at the tip of the large nose.

She considered for a moment. "I'm glad I know," she said gravely. "I wanted to, awful much."

After that she studied the bill-board for a time. And presently discovered that a second supply of eyes was displayed there, being set in it as jewels are set in brooches!

She pointed. "What kind are those?"

He looked surprised at the question. "The bill-board is the rear wall of my shop," said he. "And those eyes are wall-eyes."

She flushed with pleasure. "That's *exactly* what I thought!" she declared.

She began to walk up and down, one hand in the patch-pocket—to make sure it was really there. For this was all too good to be true. Here, in this Land so new to her, and so wonderful, were things about which she had pondered, and puzzled, and asked questions—the tongues, for instance, and the lime-lights, and the soda-water. How simply and naturally each was now explained!—explained as she herself had imagined each would be. She felt a sudden pride in herself. So far had anything been really unexpected? As she went back to pause in front of the little old gentleman, it was with a delightful sense of understanding. Oh, this was one of her pretend-games, gloriously come true!

Now she felt a very flood of questions surge to her lips. She pointed to a deep yellow bowl set on the table beside him. "Would you mind telling me what that is?" she asked.

"That? That's a sauce-box." And he smiled.

"Oh!—What's it full of, please?"

"Full of mouths,"—cheerily.

It was her turn to smile. She smiled into the sauce-box. At its center was a queer object, very like a short length of dried apple-peeling.

"I s'pose that's part of a mouth?" she ventured.

He picked up the object and balanced it across his thumb. "You've guessed it!" he declared. "And it's a fine thing to carry around with one. You see, it's a stiff upper lip." He tossed it back.

"My!" She took a deep breath. "Once I asked and *asked* about a stiff upper lip."

He went on with his polishing. "Should think you'd be more interested in these," he observed, giving a nod of the ragged hat toward a shallow dish at his elbow. "Little girls generally are."

She looked, and saw that the dish was heaped high with what seemed to be *white peanuts*—peanuts that tapered to a point at one end. She puckered her brows over them.

"Can't guess?" said he. "Then you didn't drink enough of that soda-water. Well, ever hear of a sweet tooth?"

At that she clapped her hands and jumped up and down. "Why, I've *got* one!" she cried.

"Oh?" said the little old gentleman. "Thought so. I *always* keep a supply on hand. Carve 'em myself, out of cube sugar."

"Oh, aren't they funny!" She leaned above the shallow dish.

"Funny?" repeated the Man-Who-Makes-Faces. "Not when they get into the wrong mouth!—a wry mouth, for instance, or an ugly mouth. A sweet tooth should go, you understand, only with a sweet face."

"Is it a sweet tooth that makes a face sweet?" she inquired.

"Quite so." He held up the nose to examine it critically.

She watched him in silence for a while. Then, "You don't mind telling me who's going to have that?" she ventured, pointing a finger at the nose.

"This? Oh, this is for a certain little boy's father."

She blinked thoughtfully. "Is his name," she began—and stopped.

"His father—the unfortunate man—has been keeping his own nose to the grindstone pretty steadily of late, and so—"

"I can't just remember the name I'm thinking about," said Gwendolyn, troubled.

He glanced up. And the round, bright eyes were grave as he searched her face. "I wonder," he said in a low voice, "if you know who *you* are."

She smiled. "Well, I've been acquainted with myself for seven years," she declared.

"But do you know who you *are?*" (The round eyes were full of tears!)

She felt uncertain. "I did just a little while ago. Now, though—"

He reached to take her hand. "Shall I tell you?"

"Yes,"—in a whisper.

"You're the Poor Little Rich Girl." He patted her hand. "The Poor Little Rich Girl!"

She nodded bravely, and stood looking up at him. He was old and unkempt. Out at elbows, too. And the bottoms of his baggy trousers hung in dusty shreds. But his lined and bearded face was kind! "I—I haven't been so very happy," she said falteringly.

He shook his head. "Not happy! And no step-relations, either!"

"Well,—er," (she felt uncertain) "there are some step-houses just across the street."

"Not the same thing," he declared shortly. "But, *hm! hm!*"—as he coughed, he waved an arm cheerily. "Things will improve. Oh, yes. All you've got to do is follow my advice."

The gray eyes were wistful, and questioning.

"You've got a lot to do," he went on. "Oh, a *great* deal. For instance"—here he paused, running his fingers through his long hair—"there's Miss Royle, and Thomas, and Jane."

She was silent for a long moment. Miss Royle! Thomas! Jane! In the joy of being out of doors, of having real dirt to scuff in, and high grass through which to brush; of having a plaid gingham with a pocket, and all the fizzing drink she wished; of being able to dabble and wade; and of having good, squashy soda-mud for pies—in the joy at all this she had utterly forgotten them!

She looked up at the tapered trees, and down at the flower-bordered ground; then at the bill-board, and the loaded tables of that marvelous establishment. There was still so much to see! And, oh, how many scores of questions to ask!

He bent until his beard swept the sauce-box. "You'll just have to keep out of their *clutches*," he declared.

Again she nodded, twisting and untwisting her fingers. "I thought maybe they didn't come here."

"Come?" he grunted. "Won't they be hunting *you?* Well, keep out of their clutches, I say. That's absolutely necessary. You'll see why—if you let 'em get you! For—how'll you ever find your father?"

"*Oh!*" A sudden flush swept her face. She looked at the ground. She had forgotten Miss Royle and Thomas and Jane. Worse! Until that moment *she had forgotten her father and mother!*

"There's that harness of his," went on the Man-Who-Makes-Faces. He thought a moment, pursing his lips and twiddling his thumbs. "We'll have to consider how we can get rid of it."

She glanced up. "Where does he come?" she asked huskily; "my fath-er?"

"Um! Yes, where?" He seemed uneasy; scratched his jaw; and rearranged a row of chins. "Well, the fact is, he comes here to—er—buy candles that burn at both ends."

"Of course. Is it far?"

"Out in a new fashionable addition—yes, addition, subtraction, multiplication."

"*You* won't mind showing me the way?" Now her face grew pale with earnestness.

He smiled sadly. "I? Your father thinks poorly of me. He's driven me off the block once or twice, you know. Though"—he looked away thoughtfully—"when you come to think of it there isn't such a lot of difference between your father and me. He makes money: I make faces."

It was one of those unpleasant moments when there seemed very little to be said. She stood on the other foot.

He began polishing once more. "Then there's that bee," he resumed—

"Moth-er."

He went on as quickly as possible. "Of course there are lots of things worse than one of those so-cial hon-ey-gath-er-ing in-sects—"

"She sees nothing else! She *hears* nothing else!"

"Um! We'll help her get rid of it!—*if!*"

"If?"

"You've got a lot to overcome. Recollect the Policeman?"

She retreated a step.

"Just suppose we meet *him!* And the Bear that—"

"My!"

"Yes. And a certain Doctor."

"Oh, *dear!*"

"Bad! Pretty bad!"

"Where does my moth-er come?"—timidly.

The question embarrassed. "Er—the place is full of carriage-lamps," he began; "and—and side-lights, and search-lights, and—er—lanterns."

She looked concerned. "I can't guess."

"Just ordinary lanterns," he added. "You see, the Madam comes to—to Robin Hood's Barn."

"Robin Hood's Barn!"

"Exactly. Nice day, *isn't* it?"

By the expression on his face, Gwendolyn judged that Robin Hood's Barn —of which she had often heard—was a most undesirable spot. "Is it far?" she asked, swallowing.

"No. Only—we'll have to go around it."

Somehow, all at once, he seemed the one friend she had. She put out a hand to him. "You *will* go with me?" she begged. "Oh, I want to find my fath-er, and my moth-er!"

"You want to tell 'em the real truth about those three servants they're hiring. Unless I'm *much* mistaken, your parents have never taken one good square look at those three."

"Oh, let's start." Now, of a sudden, all the hopes and plans of the past months came crowding back into her mind. "I want to sit at the grown-up table," she declared. "And I want to live in the country, and go to day-school."

He hung the hand-organ over a shoulder. "You can do every one of them," he said, "if we find your father and mother."

"We'll find them," she cried determinedly.

"We'll find 'em," he said, "if, as we go along, we don't leave one—single—stone—*unturned*."

"Oh!" she glanced about her, searching the ground.

"Not *one*," he repeated. "And now—we'll start." He picked up two or three small articles—an ear, a handful of hair, a plump cheek.

"But there's a stone right here," said Gwendolyn. It was a small one, and lay at her feet, close to the table-leg.

He peered over. "All right! Turn it!"

She stooped—turned the rock—straightened.

The next moment a chill swept her; the next, she felt a heavy hand upon her shoulder, and clumsy fingers busy with the buttons on the gingham dress.

"*Tee! hee! hee! hee!*"

It was the voice that had called from a distance. Hearing it now she felt a sudden, sickish, sinking feeling. She whirled.

A strange creature was kneeling behind her—a creature dressed in black sateen, and like no human being that she had ever met before. For it was *two-faced!*

One face (the front) was blowzy and freckled, with a small pug nose and a quarrelsome mouth. The other (the face on what, with ordinary persons, was the back of the head) was dark and forbidding, its nose a large brick-colored pug, the mouth underneath shaped most extraordinarily—not unlike a *barrette*, for it was wide and long, and square at the corners, and full of shining tortoise-shell teeth! But the creature had only one tongue. This was loose at both ends, so that there was one tip for her front face, and one for the back. But she had only one pair of eyes. These were reddish. They watched Gwendolyn boldly from the front; then rolled quickly to the rear to stare at the Man-Who-Makes-Faces.

At sight of the two-faced creature, Gwendolyn shrank away, frightened.

"Oh!—oh, my!" she faltered.

Both horrid mouths now bellowed hilariously. And the creature reached out a big hand.

"Look here, Gwendolyn!" it ordered. "You ain't goin'!"

Gwendolyn lifted terrified eyes for a second look at the brick-colored hair, the blowzy countenance. No possibility of doubt remained!

CHAPTER IX

Bobbing and swaying foolishly, the nurse-maid shuffled to her feet. And Gwendolyn, though she wanted to turn and flee beyond the reach of those big, clutching hands, found herself rooted to the ground, and could only stand and stare helplessly.

The Man-Who-Makes-Faces stepped to her side hastily. His look was perturbed. "My! My!" he exclaimed under his breath. "She's worse than I thought!—*much* worse."

With a little gasp of relief at having him so near, Gwendolyn slipped her trembling fingers into his. "She's worse than *I* thought," she managed to whisper back.

Neither was given a chance to say more. For seeing them thus, hand in hand, Jane suddenly started forward—with a great boisterous hop and skip. Her front face was distorted with a jealous scowl. She gave Gwendolyn a rough sidewise shove.

"Git away from that old beggar!" she commanded harshly. "Why, he'll kidnap you! Look at his knife!"

Nimbly the little old gentleman thrust himself in front of her, barring her way, and shielding Gwendolyn. "Who told you where she was?" he asked angrily.

"Who?" mocked Jane, impudently. "Well, who is it that tells people things?"

"You mean the *Bird?*"

Jane's front face broke into a pleased grin. "I mean the Bird," she bragged And balanced from foot to foot.

Gwendolyn, peeking round at her, of a sudden felt a fresh concern. The Bird!—the same Bird that had repeated tales against her father! And now he was tattling on her! She saw all her hopes of finding her parents, all her happy plans, in danger of being blighted.

"Oh, my goodness!" she said mournfully.

She was holding tight to the little old gentleman's coat-tails. Now he leaned down. "We *must* get rid of her," he declared. "You know what I said. She'll make us trouble!"

"Here! None of that!" It was Jane once more, the grin replaced by a dark look. "I'll have you know this child is in *my* charge." Again she tried to seize Gwendolyn.

The Man-Who-Makes-Faces stood his ground resolutely—and swung the curved knife up to check any advance.

"She doesn't need you," he declared "She's seven, and she's grown-up." And to Gwendolyn, "*Tell* her so! Don't be afraid! Tell her!"

Gwendolyn promptly opened her mouth. But try as she would, she could not speak. Her lips seemed dry. Her tongue refused to move. She could only swallow!

As if he understood her plight, the little old gentleman suddenly sprang aside to where was the sauce-box, snatched something out of it, ran to the other table and picked up an oblong leather case (a case exactly like the gold-mounted one in which Miss Royle kept her spectacles), put the something out of the sauce-box into the case, closed the case with a snap, and put it, with a swift motion, into Gwendolyn's hand.

"There!" he cried triumphantly. "There's that stiff upper lip! *Now* you can answer."

It was true! No sooner did she feel the leather case against her palm, than her fear, and her hesitation and lack of words, were gone!

She assumed a determined attitude, and went up to Jane. "I don't need you," she said firmly. "'Cause I'm seven years old now, and I'm grown up. And— what are you here for *anyhow?*"

At the very boldness of it, Jane's manner completely changed. That front countenance took on a silly simper. And she put her two-faced head, now on one side, now on the other, ingratiatingly.

"What am I here for!" she repeated in an injured tone. "And you ask me that, Miss? Why, what *should* I be doin' for you, lovie, but dancin' attendance."

At that, she began to act most curiously, stepping to the right and pointing a toe, stepping to the left and pointing a toe; setting down one heel, setting down the other; then taking a waltzing turn.

"Oh!" said Gwendolyn, understanding. (For dancing attendance was precisely what Jane was doing!) After observing the other's antics for a moment, she tossed her head. "Well, if *that's* all you want to do," she said unconcernedly, "why, *dance*."

"Yes, dance," broke in the Man-Who-Makes-Faces, snapping his fingers. "Frolic and frisk and flounce!"

Jane obeyed. And waltzed up to the bill-board. "Say! what's the price of that big braid?" she called—between her tortoise-shell teeth. She had spied the red coronet, and was admiring its plaited beauty.

From under those long, square brows, the little old gentleman frowned across the table at her. "I'll quote you no prices," he answered. "You haven't paid me yet for your extra face."

Jane's reply was an impudent double-laugh. She was examining the different things on the bill-board, and hopping sillily from foot to foot.

Gwendolyn tugged gently at a coat-tail. "Can't we run now?" she asked; "and hide?"

Boom-er-oom-er-oom!

"Sh!" warned the Man-Who-Makes-Faces, not stirring. "What was that!"

"I don't know."

Both held their breath. And Gwendolyn took a more firm hold of the lip-case.

After a moment the little old gentleman began to speak very low: "We shan't be able to steal away. She's watching us out of the back of her head!"

"Yes. I can see 'em shine!"

"I believe that when she rolled her eyes from one face to the other it made that *rumbley sound*."

"Scares me," whispered Gwendolyn.

"Ump!" he grunted. "Ought to cheer you up. For it's my opinion that her eyes rumble *because her head's empty*."

"If it was hollow I think I'd know," she answered doubtfully. "You see she's been my nurse a long time. But—would it help?"

"*Find out*," he advised. "And if it's a fact, your mother ought to know."

Boom-er-oom-er-oom!

Gwendolyn, watching, saw two shining spots in Jane's back face grow suddenly small—to the size of glinting pin-points; then disappear. The nurse turned, and came dancing back.

"You'd better let me have that braid, old man," she cried rudely.

"I'll smooth down your saucy tongue," he threatened.

"Tee! hee! hee! hee!" she tittered. "Ha! ha! ha!"

Gwendolyn had heard her laugh before. But it was the first time she had *seen* her laugh. The Man-Who-Makes-Faces, too. Now, at the same moment, both witnessed an extraordinary thing: As Jane chuckled, she lifted one stout arm so that a black sateen cuff was close to the mouth of the front face. And holding it there, actually *laughed in her sleeve!*

Laughed in her sleeve—*and a great deal more!* For with each chuckle, from the top of her red head to her very feet, *she grew a trifle more plump!*

The little old gentleman warned her with one long finger. "You look out, young lady!" said he. "One of these days you'll laugh on the other side of your face." (Which made Gwendolyn wish that it was not impolite to correct those older than herself; for it was plain that he meant "you'll laugh on your *other* face.")

Jane put out a tongue-tip at him insolently. Then dancing near, "Come!" she bade Gwendolyn. "Come away with Nurse."

The Man-Who-Makes-Faces made no effort to interpose. But he wagged his head significantly. "It's evident, Miss Jane," said he, "that you've forgotten all about—the Piper."

She came short. And showed herself upset by what he had said, for she did a hop-schottische.

He was not slow to take advantage. "We're sure to see him shortly," he went on. "And when we do—! Because your account with him is adding up *terrifically*. You're dancing a good deal, you know."

"How can I help *that?*" demanded Jane. "Ain't I dancin' atten—"

Gwendolyn forgot to listen to the remainder of the sentence. All at once she was a little apprehensive on her own account—remembering how *she* had danced beside the soda-water, not half an hour before!

"Mr. Man-Who-Makes-Faces," she began timidly, "do you mean the Piper that everybody has to pay?"

"Exactly," replied the little old gentleman. "He's out collecting some pay for me now—from a dishonest fellow who didn't settle for two dozen ears that I boxed and sent him."

At that, Jane began tittering harder than ever (hysterically, this time), holding up her arm as before—and filling out two or three wrinkles in the black sateen! And Gwendolyn, watching closely, saw that while the front face of her nurse was all a-grin, the face on the back of her head wore a nervous expression. (Evidently that front face was not always to be depended upon!)

The little old gentleman also remarked the nervous expression. And followed up the advantage already won. "Now," said he, "perhaps you'll be willing to come along quietly. We're just starting, you understand." He jerked a thumb over his shoulder.

Gwendolyn glanced in the direction he pointed. And saw—for the first time —that a wide, smooth road led away from the Face-Shop, a road as wide and smooth and curving as the Drive. Like the Drive it was well-lighted on either side (but lighted low-down) by a row of tiny electric bulbs with frosted shades, each resembling an incandescent toadstool. (She remembered having once caught a glimpse of something similar in a store-window.) These tiny lamps were set close together on short stems, precisely as white stones of a selected size edged all the paths at Johnnie Blake's. And each gave out a soft light. She did not have to ask about them. She guessed promptly what they were—lights to make plain the way for people's feet: in short, nothing more nor less than footlights!

A few times in her life—so few that she could tell them off on her pink fingers—she had been taken to the theater, Jane accompanying her by right of nurse-maid, Miss Royle by her superior right as judge of all matters that partook of entertainment; Thomas coming also, though apparently for no reason whatever, to grace a rear seat along with the chauffeur. Seated in a box, close to the curved edge of the stage, she had seen the soft glow of the footlights. But for some reason which she could not fathom, the footlights had always been carefully concealed from everyone but the people on the stage. Trying to imagine them without any suggestions from Miss Royle or Jane, she had patterned them after a certain stuffed slipper-cushion that stood on Jane's dressing-table. How different was the reality, and how much more satisfactory!

Jane looked up the road, between the lines of footlights. "You're just startin'," she repeated. "Where?"

"To find her father and mother," answered the Man-Who-Makes-Faces, stoutly.

At that Jane shook her huge pompadour. "Father and mother!" she cried. "Indeed, you won't! Not while *I'm* a-takin' care of her." And reaching out, caught Gwendolyn—by a slender wrist.

The Man-Who-Makes-Faces seized the other. And the next moment Gwendolyn was unpleasantly reminded of times in the nursery, times when, Miss Royle and Jane disagreeing about her, each pulled at an arm and quarreled. For here was the nurse, tugging one direction to drag her away, and the little old gentleman tugging the other with all his might.

"Slap her hands! Slap her hands!" he shouted excitedly. "It'll start circulation."

Both slapped—so hard that her hands stung. And with the result he sought. For instantly all three began going in circles, around and around, faster and faster and faster.

It was Jane who first let go. She was puffing hard, and the perspiration was standing out upon her forehead. "I'm going to call the Policeman," she threatened shrilly.

"Oh! Oh! Please don't!" Gwendolyn's cry was as shrill. "I don't want him to get me!"

"*Call* the Policeman then," retorted the Man-Who-Makes-Faces. And to Gwendolyn, soothingly, "Hush! Hush, child!"

Jane danced away—sidewise, as if to keep watch as she went. "Help! Help!" she shouted. "Police! Police!! *Poli-i-i-ice!!!*"

Gwendolyn was terribly frightened. But she could not run. One wrist was still in the grasp of the little old gentleman. With wildly throbbing heart she watched the road.

"Is he coming?" called the little old gentleman. He, too, was looking up the curving road.

A whistle sounded. It was long-drawn, piercing.

And now Gwendolyn heard movements all about her in the forest—the soft *pad, pad* of running paws, the *hushing* sound of wings—as if small live things were fleeing before the sharp call.

Jane hastened back, galloping a polka. "Turn a stone! Turn a stone!" she cried, rumbling her eyes.

Gwendolyn clung to the little old gentleman. "Oh, don't let her!" she plead. "What if—"

"We *must*."

"Will a pebble-size do?" yelled Jane, excitedly.

"Yes! Yes!" answered the Man-Who-Makes-Faces. "You've seen stones in rings, haven't you? Aren't *they* pebble-size?"

The nurse stooped, picked up a small stone, and sent it spinning from the end of a thumb.

Faint with fear, Gwendolyn thrust a trembling hand into the patch-pocket and took hold of the lip-case. Then leaning against the little old gentleman, her yellow head half-concealed by the dusty flap of his torn coat, she waited.

CHAPTER X

What she first saw was a face!—straight ahead, at the top of a steep rise, where the wide road narrowed to a point. The face was a man's, and upon it the footlights beat so strongly that each feature was startlingly vivid. But it was not the fact that she saw *only* a face that set her knees to trembling weakly—nor the fact that the face was fearfully distorted; but because it was *upside down!*

She stared, feeling herself grow cold, her flesh creep. "Oh, I want to go home!" she gasped.

The face began to move nearer, slowly, inch by inch. And there sounded a hoarse outcry: "*Hoo! hoo! Hoo! hoo!*"

It was the little old gentleman who reassured her somewhat—by his even voice. "Ah!" said he with something of pride, yet as if to himself. "He realizes that the black eye is a beauty. And I shouldn't wonder if he isn't coming to match it!"

But what temporary confidence she gained, fled when Jane, tettering from side to side, began to threaten in a most terrifying way. "*Now*, young Miss!" she cried. "*Now*, you're goin' to be sorry you didn't mind Jane! Oh, *I* told you he'd git you some fine day!"

The Man-Who-Makes-Faces retorted—what, Gwendolyn did not hear. She was sick with apprehension. "I guess I won't find my father and moth-er now," she whispered miserably.

Then, all at once, she could see *more* than a face! Silhouetted against the lighted sky was a figure—broad shouldered and belted, with swinging cudgel, and visored cap. It was like those dreaded figures that patroled the Drive—yet how different! For as the Policeman came on, his wild face peered between his coat-tails!—peered between his coat-tails for the reason that he was *upside down*, and walking *on his hands!*

"*Hoo! hoo!* Hoo! hoo!" he clamored again. His coat flopped about his ears. His natural merino socks showed where his trousers fell away from his shoes. His club bumped the side of his head at every stride of his long blue-clad arms.

His identification was complete. For precisely as Thomas had declared, he was *heels over head.*

"My!" breathed Gwendolyn, so astonished that she almost forgot to be anxious for her own safety. (What a marvelous Land was this—where everything was really as it ought to be!)

The Man-Who-Makes-Faces addressed her, smiling down. "You won't mind if we don't start for a minute or two, will you?" he inquired. "This Officer will probably want to discuss the prices of eyes. You see, I gave him his black one. If he wants another, though, I shall be obliged to ask the Piper to collect."

"Aren't—aren't you afraid of him?" stammered Gwendolyn, in a whisper.

"*Afraid?*" he echoed, surprised. "Why, no! Are *you?*"

Somehow, she felt ashamed. "N-n-not very," she faltered.

No sooner did she partly deny her fear than she experienced a most delicious feeling of security! And this feeling grew as she watched the nearing Policeman. For she saw that he was in a mournful state.

It was worry and grief that distorted his face. The dark eyes above the visor (both the black eye and the other one) were streaming with tears, tears which, naturally enough, ran from the four corners of his eyes, down across his forehead, and on into his hair. And it was evident that he had been weeping for a long time, for his cap was full!

And now she realized that the hoarse cries which had filled her with terror were the saddest of complaints!—were not "Hoo! hoo!" but "*Boo!* hoo!"

"Poor man!" sympathized the little old gentleman, wagging his beard.

Jane, however, with characteristic lack of compassion, hopped about, *tee-heeing* loudly—and straightening out any number of wrinkles. "Oh, ain't he a sight!" she chortled. She had entirely given over her threatening.

Gwendolyn now felt secure enough. But she did not feel like laughing. She was sober to the point of pitying. For though he looked ridiculous, he was so absolutely helpless, so utterly unhappy.

"Oh, dear! Oh, dear!" he exclaimed as he came on—hand over hand, legs held together, and swaying from side to side rhythmically, like the pendulum of the metronome. "What shall I do! What shall I do!"

"Need any sharpening?" called out the Man-Who-Makes-Faces, brandishing the curved knife. "Is there something wrong?"

"Wrong!" echoed the Policeman dolefully. "I should say so! Oh, *dear!* Oh, dear!" And still weeping copiously, so that his forehead glistened with his tears, he plodded across the border of the Face-Shop.

It was then that Gwendolyn recalled under what circumstances she had seen him last. Only two or three days before, when bound homeward in the limousine, she had spied him loitering beside the walled walk. "What makes his club shine so?" she had asked Jane, whispering. "Eh?" whispered Jane in return; "what else than *blood?*" The wind was blowing as the automobile swept past him: The breeze lifted the tail of his belted coat. And for one terrifying instant Gwendolyn caught a glimpse of steel!

"And if he don't mean harm to anybody," Jane had added when Gwendolyn turned scared eyes to her, "why does he carry a *pistol?*"

But there was no need to fear a weapon now. The falling away of his coat-tails had uncovered his trouser-pockets. And as he halted, Gwendolyn saw that his revolver was gone, his pistol-pocket empty.

She took a timid step toward him. "How do you do, Mr. Officer," she said. "Can't you let your feet come down? Then you'd be on your back, and you could get up the right way."

Up came his face between his coat-tails. He stared at her with his new black eye—with the other one, too. (She noted that it was blue.) "But I *am* up the right way," he answered, "Oh, no! It isn't that! It isn't that!" His hands were encased in white cotton gloves. He rocked himself from one to the other.

"No, it *isn't* that," agreed the little old gentleman; "but I firmly believe that, you'd feel better if you'd order another eye."

"Another eye!" said the Policeman, bitterly. "Would another eye help me to find him?"

"Oh, I see." The Man-Who-Makes-Faces spoke with some concern. "Then he's flown?"

Gwendolyn, puzzled, glanced from one to the other. "Who is 'he'?" she asked.

The Policeman bumped his head against his night-stick. "The Bird!" he mourned.

At that, Jane hopped up and down in evident delight.

But Gwendolyn fell back, taking up a position beside the little old gentleman. That Bird again! And it was evident that the Policeman thought well of him!

Pity swiftly merged into suspicion.

"I s'pose you mean the Bird that tells people things," she ventured—to be sure that she was not misjudging him.

He wiped his black eye on a coat-tail. "Aye," he answered. "That's the one. And, oh, but he could tell *you* things!"

Gwendolyn considered the statement. At last, "He's a tattletale!" she charged, and felt her cheeks crimson with sudden anger.

He nodded—so vigorously that some of his tears splashed over the rim of his cap. "That's why the Police can't get along without him," he declared. "And, oh, here I've gone and lost him! And They'll put me off the Force!" (Bump! bump! bump!)

"They?" she questioned. "Do you mean the soda-water They?"

"And They know so much," explained the little old gentleman, "because the Bird tells 'em."

"He tells 'em everything," grumbled the Officer. "They send him around the whole country hunting gossip—when he ought to be working exclusively in the interest of Law and Order."

Law and Order—Gwendolyn wondered who these two were.

"He knows everything *I* do," asserted the Policeman, "and everything *she* does—" Here he jerked his head sidewise at Jane.

She retreated, an expression of guilt on that front face.

"And everything *you* do," he went on, indicating Gwendolyn.

"I know that," she said in an injured tone. "He told Jane I was here."

At that, the Policeman gave himself a quick half-turn. "You've *seen* him?" he demanded of the nurse.

She shifted from side to side nervously. "It ain't the same one," she protested. "It—"

He interrupted. "You couldn't be mistaken," he declared. "Did he have a bumpy forehead? and a lumpy tail?"

"You don't mean *a lump of salt*," said Gwendolyn, astonished.

"He does," said the little old gentleman. "And the bumpy forehead is from having to remember so many things."

She heaved a sigh of relief. "Well, I think I'd like *that* Bird," she said. "And I don't believe he's far. 'Cause when you whistled I heard flying."

"*Running* and flying," corrected the Policeman; "—running and flying to *me*." (He said it proudly.) "The squirrels and the robin-redbreasts, and the sparrows, all follow me here from the Park of a night, knowing I protect 'em."

"Oh?" murmured Gwendolyn. "You protect 'em?" She looked sidewise at Jane, reflecting that the nurse had given him quite another character.

"Yes; and I protect old, old people."

"Huh!" snorted the Man-Who-Makes-Faces. "You protect old people, eh? Well, how about old *organ-grinders?*"

"You ought to know," answered the Officer promptly. "I guess you didn't give me that black eye for nothing."

Whereat the little old gentleman suddenly subsided into silence.

"Yes, I protect old people," reiterated the other, "and the blind, of course, and the trees and the flowers and the fountains. Also, the statues. There's the General, for instance. If I didn't watch out, folks would scribble on him with chalk."

Gwendolyn assented. Once more she was beginning to have belief in him.

"Then," he resumed, "I look after the children, so that—"

She started. The children!—*he?* "But," she interrupted, "Jane's always told me that you grab little boys and girls *and carry 'em off.*" Then, fairly shook at her own boldness.

"I never!" denied Jane, sullenly.

He laughed. "I *do* carry 'em off. But *where?*"

"I don't know,"—in a flutter.

"Tell her," urged the little old gentleman.

The Policeman leaned his feet against the bill-board. "I'm the man," said he, "that takes lost little kids to their fathers and mothers."

To their fathers and mothers! Gwendolyn came round upon Jane, lifting accusing eyes, pointing an accusing finger, "So!" she breathed. "You told me he stole 'em! It isn't *true!*" And she wiggled the finger.

Jane edged away, head on one side "Oh, I was jokin' you," she declared lightly. But—accidentally—- she turned aside her grinning front face and gave the others a glimpse of the back one. And each noted how the square mouth was trembling with anxiety.

"Ah-ha!" exclaimed Gwendolyn, triumphantly. "I'm finding you out!"

The Policeman crossed his feet against the bill-board, taking care not to injure any of the articles there displayed. "Yes, I've taken a lot of lost little kids to their fathers and mothers," he repeated. "And I was just wondering if you—"

She gave him no chance to finish his sentence. In her joy at finding that here was another friend, she ran to him and leaned to smile into his face.

"You'll help *me* to find my fath-er and moth-er, won't you?" she cried.

"*Cer*-tainly!"

"We were starting just as you came," said the Man-Who-Makes-Faces.

"Well, let's be off!" His whistle hung by a thin chain from a button-hole of his coat. He swung it to his lips, *Toot! Toot!* It was a cheery blast.

The next moment, coming, as it were, on the heels of her sudden good fortune, Gwendolyn closed her right hand and found herself possessed of a bag of candy!—red-and-white stick-candy of the variety that she had often seen selling at street corners (out of show-cases that went on wheels). More than once she had longed, and in vain, to stop at one of these show-cases and purchase. Now she suddenly remembered having done so with a high hand. The sticks were striped spirally. Boldly she produced one and fell to sucking it, making more noise with her sucking than ever the strict proprieties of the nursery permitted.

Then, candy in hand, and with the little old gentleman on her right, the Policeman on her left, and Jane trailing behind, doing a one-two-three-and-point, she set forward gayly along the wide, curving road.

CHAPTER XI

As she trotted along, pulling with great relish at a candy-stick, she glanced down at the Policeman every now and then—and glowed with pride. On some few well-remembered occasions her chauffeur had condescended to hold a short conversation with her; had even permitted her to sound the clarion of the limousine, with its bright, piercing tones. All of which had been keenly gratifying. But here she was, actually conversing with an Officer in full uniform! And on terms of perfect equality!

She proffered him the bag of spiral sweets.

He cocked his head side wise at it. "Is that the chewing kind?" he inquired.

"Oh, I'm sorry!"

However, he did not seem in the least disappointed. For he had a mouthful of gum, and this he cracked loudly from time to time—in a way that excited her admiration and envy.

"I've watched you go by our house lots of times," she confided presently, eager to say something cordial.

"Oh?" said he. "It's a beat that does well enough in summer. But in the wintertime I'd rather be Down-Town." Puffing a little,—for though he was upside down and walking on his hands, he had so far made good progress— he halted and rested his feet against the lowest limb of a tree that stood close to the road. Now his cap touched the ground, and his hands were free. With one white-gloved finger he drew three short lines in the packed dirt.

"And you *ought* to be Down-Town," declared the little old gentleman, halting too. "Because you're a Policeman with a level head."

A level head? Gwendolyn stooped to look. And saw that it was indeed a fact!

"If I hadn't one," answered the Policeman with dignity, "would I be able to stand up comfortably in this remarkable manner?"

"Oh, tee! hee! hee! hee!"

It was the nurse, her sleeve lifted, her blowzy face convulsed. As she laughed, Gwendolyn saw wrinkle after wrinkle in the black sateen taken up —with truly alarming rapidity.

"My!" she exclaimed. "Jane's always been stout. But now—!"

The Policeman was deepening the three short lines in the dirt, making a capital A. "Two streets come together," he said, placing his finger on the point of the letter. "And the block that connects 'em just before they meet, that's the beat for *me*."

"I hope you'll get it," she said heartily.

"Get it!" he repeated bitterly. "Well, I certainly won't if I don't find that Bird!" And he started forward once more.

The Man-Who-Makes-Faces, trudging alongside, craned to peer ahead, his grizzled beard sticking straight out in front of him. "Now, let me see," he mused in a puzzled way. "Which route, I wonder, had we better take?"

"That depends on where we're going," replied the Policeman, helplessly. "And with the Bird gone, of course I don't know."

"I'll tell you," said the little old gentleman promptly. "First, we must cross the Glass—"

Gwendolyn gave him a quick glance. Surely he meant cross the *grass*.

"Yes, the Glass; go on," encouraged the Officer.

"—And find *him*." Those round dark eyes darted a quick glance at Gwendolyn.

Jane, capering at his heels, now interrupted. "Find him!" she taunted. "Gwendolyn'll never find her father if she don't listen to me."

He ignored her. "Next," he went on "we'll steer straight for Robin Hood's Barn."

"Oh!" exclaimed the Policeman "Then we have to go around."

"*Every*body has to go around."

Once more Jane broke in. "Gwendolyn," she called, "you'll never find your mother. This precious pair is takin' you the wrong way!"

Gwendolyn paid no heed. Ahead the road divided—to the left in a narrow bridle-path, all loose soil and hoof-prints, and sharp turns; to the right in a level thoroughfare that held a straight course. She touched the little old gentleman's elbow. "Which?" she whispered.

As the parting of the ways was reached, he pointed. And she saw a sign—a sign with an arrow directing travelers to the right. Under the arrow, plainly lettered, were the words:

Gwendolyn looked her concern. "Do we *have* to go that road?" she asked him.

He nodded.

The next moment, with a loud rumbling of the eyes, Jane came alongside. "Oh, dearie," she cried, "you couldn't hire *me* to go. And I wouldn't like to see *you* go. I think too much of you, I do *indeed*."

"Hold your tongue!" ordered the little old gentleman, crossly.

Jane obeyed. Up came a hand, and she seized the tongue-tip in her front mouth. But since there was a second tongue-tip in that back face, she still continued her babbling: "Don't ask me to trapse over the hard pavements on my poor tired feet, dearie, just because you take your notions.... Come, I say! Your mother's nobody, anyhow.... You don't know what you're sayin' or doin', poor thing! You're just wanderin', that's all—just wanderin'."

"I'm wandering in the right direction, anyhow," retorted Gwendolyn, stoutly. And to the little old gentleman, "I'm sorry we're going this way, though. I'm 'fraid of Bears,"—for the sign was past now; the four were on the level thoroughfare.

The Policeman seemed not to have remarked her anxiety. "And after the Den, what do we pass?" he questioned.

"The Big Rock," answered the Man-Who-Makes-Faces.

"Do we have to turn it?" The other spoke with some annoyance. "What's likely to come out? I suppose it won't be hiding that Bird."

"There's a hollow under the Rock," said the little old gentleman. "We'll find *something*." His face grew grave.

"And—and after we go by the Big Rock?" ventured Gwendolyn.

The little old gentleman smiled. "Ah, then!" he said, "—then we come to the Pillery!"

"Oh!" She considered the reply. Pillery—it was a word she had never chanced upon in the large Dictionary. Yet she felt she could hardly ask any questions about it. She had asked so many already. "It's kind of you to answer and answer and answer," she said aloud. "Nobody else ever did that."

"Ask anything you want to know," he returned cordially. "I'll always give you prompt attention. Though of course, there are *some* things—" He hesitated.

"Yes?"—eagerly.

"That only fathers and mothers can answer."

"Oh!"

"Didn't you know that?" demanded the Policeman, surprised.

"Tee! hee! hee! hee!" snickered Jane. Though she was some few steps in the rear, her difficult breathing could be plainly heard. She had laughed so much into her sleeve, and had grown so stout, that by now not a single wrinkle remained in the black sateen; *worse*—she was beginning to try every square inch of the cloth sorely. And having danced every foot of the way, she was tiring.

"Oh, fath-er-and-moth-er questions," said Gwendolyn.

"Precisely," answered the little old gentleman; "—about my friends, Santa Claus and the Sand-Man, for instance—"

"They're not friends of Potter's, I guess. 'Cause he—"

"—And the fairies, and the gnomes, and the giants; and Mother Goose and *her* crowd. Of course a nurse or a governess or a teacher of some sort might *try* to explain. Wouldn't do any good, though. You wouldn't understand."

The Policeman swung his head back and forth, nodding. "That's the worst," said he, "of being a Poor—" Here he fell suddenly silent, and spatted the dust with his palms in an embarrassed way.

She understood. "A Poor Little Rich Girl," she said, "who doesn't see her fath-er and moth-er."

"But you will," he declared determinedly, and forged ahead faster than ever, white hand following white hand.

It was then that Gwendolyn heard the nurse muttering and chortling to herself. "Well, I never!" exclaimed the tongue-tip that was not being held. "If this ain't a' *automobile* road! Why, it's a *fine* auto*mo*bile road! Ha! ha! ha! *That makes a difference!*"

Gwendolyn was startled. What did Jane mean? *What* difference? Why so much satisfaction all at once? She wished the others would listen; would take note of the triumphant air. But both were busy, the little old gentleman chattering and pointing ahead, the Policeman straining to keep pace and look where his companion directed.

To lessen her uneasiness, Gwendolyn hunted a second stick of candy. Then sidled in between her two friends. "Oh, please," she began appealingly, with a glance up and a glance down, "I'm 'fraid Jane's going to make us trouble. Can't we think of some way to get rid of her?"

The Policeman twisted his neck around until he could wink at her with his black eye. "In town," said he meaningly, "we Policemen have a way."

"Oh, tell us!" she begged. For the Man-Who-Makes-Faces looked keenly interested.

"Well," resumed the Officer—and now he halted just long enough to raise a gloved finger to one side of his head with a significant gesture—"when we want to get rid of a person, we put a flea in his ear."

Gwendolyn blushed rosy. A flea! It was an insect that Miss Royle had never permitted her to mention. Still—

"But—but where could we—er—find—a—a—?"

She had stammered that far when she saw the little old gentleman turn his wrinkled face over a shoulder. Next, he jerked an excited thumb. And looking, she saw that Jane was *failing to keep up.*

By now the nurse had swelled to astonishing proportions. Her body was as round as a barrel. Her face was round too, and more red than ever. Her cheeks were so puffed, the skin of her forehead was so tight and shiny, that she looked precisely like a monster copy of a sanitary rubber doll!

"She can't last much longer! Her strength's giving out." It was the Policeman. And his voice ended in a sob. (Yet the sob meant nothing, for he was showing all his white teeth in a delighted smile.)

"She must have help!"—this the Man-Who-Makes-Faces. His voice broke, too. But his round, dark eyes were brimming with laughter.

"Who'll help her?" demanded Gwendolyn. "*Nobody*. So *one* of that three is gone for good!"

She halted now—on the summit of a rise. Up this, but at a considerable distance, Jane was toiling, with feeble hops to the right, and staggering steps to the left, and faint, fat gasps.

"Oh, Gwendolyn darlin'!" she called weepingly. "Oh, don't leave your Jane! Oh! Oh!"

"I've made up my mind," announced Gwendolyn, "to have the nurse-maid in the brick house. So, good-by—good-by."

She began to descend rapidly, with the little old gentleman in a shuffling run, and the Policeman springing from hand to hand as if he feared pursuit, and swaying his legs from side to side with a *tick-tock, tick-tock*. The going was easy. Soon the bottom of the slope was reached. Then all stopped to look back.

Jane had just gained the top. But was come to a standstill. Over the brow of the hill could be seen only her full face—like a big red moon.

At the sight, Gwendolyn felt a thrill of joy—the joy of freedom found again. "Why, she's not coming up," she called out delightedly. "She's going down!" And she punctuated her words with a gay skip.

That skip proved unfortunate. For as ill-luck would have it, she stumbled. And stumbling stubbed her toe. The toe struck two small stones that lay partly embedded in the road—dislodged them—turned them end for end—and sent them skimming along the ground.

"*Two!*" cried the Policeman. "*Now* who?"

"If only the right kind come!" added the little old gentleman, each of his round eyes rimmed with sudden white.

"I'll blow my whistle." Up swung the shining bit of metal on the end of its chain.

"Blow it at the top of your lungs!"

The Policeman had balanced himself on his head, thrown away his gum, and put the whistle against his lips. Now he raised it and placed it against his chest, just above his collar-button. Then he blew. And through the forest the blast rang and echoed and boomed—until all the tapers rose and fell, and all the footlights flickered.

Instantly that red moon sank below the crest of the hill. Puffs of smoke rose in its place. Then there was borne to the waiting trio a sound of *chugging*. And the next instant, with a purr of its engine, and a whirr of its wheels, here into full sight shot forward the limousine!

Gwendolyn paled. The half-devoured stick of candy slipped from her fingers. "Oh, I don't want to be shut up in the car!" she cried out. "And I won't! I *won't!* I WON'T!" She scurried behind the Man-Who-Makes-Faces.

The automobile came on. Its polished sides reflected the varied lights of the forest. Its hated windows glistened. One door swung wide, as if yawning for a victim!

The little old gentleman, as he watched it, seemed interested rather than apprehensive. After a moment, "Recollect my speaking of the Piper?" he asked.

"Y-y-yes."

At the mention of the Piper, the Policeman stared up. "The Pip-Piper!" he protested, stammering, and beginning to back away.

At that, Gwendolyn felt renewed anxiety. "The Piper!" she faltered. "Oh, I'll have to settle with him." And thrust a searching hand into the patch-pocket.

The Policeman kept on retreating. "I don't want to see him," he declared. "He made me pay too dear for my whistle." And he bumped his head against his night-stick.

The Man-Who-Makes-Faces hastened to him, and halted him by grasping him about his fast-swaying legs. "You can't run away from the Piper," he reminded. "So—"

Gwendolyn was no longer frightened. In her search for money she had found the gold-mounted leather case. This she now clutched, receiving courage from the stiff upper-lip.

But the Policeman was far from sanguine. Now perspiration and not tears glistened on his forehead. He grasped his club with one shaking hand.

As for the little old gentleman, he held the curved knife out in front of him, all his thin fingers wound tightly around its hilt. "What's the Piper got beside him?" he asked in a tone full of wonder. "Is it a *rubber-plant?*"

Gwendolyn looked. The Piper was leaning over the steering-wheel of the car. He was so near by now that she could make him out clearly—a lanky, lean-jawed young man in a greasy cap and Johnnie Blake overalls. Over his right shoulder, on a strap, was suspended a bundle. A tobacco-pipe hung from a corner of his mouth. But it was evidently not this pipe that had given him his title; but pipes of a different kind—all of lead, in varying lengths. These were arranged about his waist, somewhat like a long, uneven fringe. And among them was a pipe-wrench, a coupling or two, and a cutter.

Beside him on the seat, in the foot man's place, was a queer object. It was tall, and dark-blue in color. (Or was it green?) On one side of it were what seemed to be seven long leaves. On the other side were seven similar leaves. And as the car rolled swiftly up, these fourteen long leaf-like projections waved gently.

She had no chance to examine the object further. Something else claimed her attention. The windowed door of the limousine suddenly swung wide, and through it, toward her, was extended a long black beckoning arm. Next, a freckled face filled the whole of the opening, spying this way and that. It was Jane!

"Come, dearie," she cooed. (She had let go the front tongue-tip.) "I wouldn't stay with them two any more. Here's your beautiful car, love. *This* is what'll take you fast to your papa and mamma."

"*No!*" cried Gwendolyn. And to the Man-Who-Makes-Faces, "She was 'fraid of the Piper just a little while ago. Now, she's riding around with him. *I* think he's—"

"Ssh!" warned the little old gentleman, speaking low. "We have to have him. And he has his good points."

The Piper was staring at Gwendolyn impertinently. Now he climbed down from his seat, all his pipes *tinkling* and *tankling* as he moved, and gave her a mocking salute, quite as if he knew her—yet without removing the tobacco-pipe from between his lips, or the greasy cap from his hair.

"Well, if here ain't the P.L.R.G.," he exclaimed rudely.

As she got a better view of him she remembered that she *had* met him before—in her nursery, that fortunate morning the hot-water pipe burst. He was the very Piper that had been called in to make plumbing repairs!

"Good-evening," said Gwendolyn, nodding courteously—but staying close to the little old gentleman. For Jane had summoned strength enough to topple out of the limousine and teeter forward. Now she was kneeling in the road, crooking a coaxing finger, and gurgling invitingly.

The Piper scowled at the nurse. "Say! What do you think you're doin'?" he demanded. "Singin' a duet with yourself?" Then turning upon the Policeman, "Off your beat, ain't you?" he inquired impudently; when, without waiting for an answer, he swung round upon the Man-Who-Makes-Faces. "Old gent," he began tauntingly, "I can't collect real money for that dozen ears." And threw out an arm toward the object on the driver's seat.

Gwendolyn looked a second time. And saw a horrid and unnatural sight. For the object was a man, straight enough, broad-shouldered enough, with arms and legs, feet and hands, and a small head; but a man shockingly disfigured. For down either side of him, projecting from head and shoulders and arms, were ears—long, hairy, mulish ears, that wriggled horribly, one moment unfolding themselves to catch every sound, the next flopping about ridiculously.

"Why, he's all ears!" she gasped.

The little old gentleman started forward. "It's that dozen I boxed!" he announced. "Hey! Come out of there!"

Gwendolyn's heart sank. Now she knew. From the first her fear had been that one of the dreaded three would come and fetch her out of the Land before she could find her parents. And here, at the very moment when she hoped to leave the worst of the trio behind, here was another!—to hamper and tattle and thwart.

For the rubber plant was Thomas!

And now all at once there was the greatest excitement. The Man-Who-Makes-Faces seized Thomas by an ear and dragged him to the ground, all the while upbraiding him loudly. And while these two were occupied, the Piper swaggered toward the Policeman, his pipes and implements striking and jangling together.

"I want my money," he bellowed.

"I don't owe you anything!" retorted the Policeman.

All this gave Jane the opportunity she wished. She advanced upon Gwendolyn. "Come, sweetie," she wheedled. "Rich little girls don't hike along the streets like common poor little girls. So jump in, and pretend you're a Queen, and have a grand ride—"

Now all of a sudden a terrible inclination to obey seized Gwendolyn. There yawned that door—here burned those reddish eyes, compelling her forward into a dreaded grasp—

She screamed, covering her face.

In that moment of danger it was the Policeman who came to her rescue. Eluding the Piper, he ran, hand over hand, to the side of the car, balanced himself on his level head, and waved his club.

"Move on!" he ordered in a deep voice (precisely as Gwendolyn had heard officers order at crowded crossings); "move on, there!"

The limousine obeyed! With no one touching the steering-gear, the engine began to *chug*, the wheels to whirr. And purring again, like some great good-natured live thing, it gained momentum, took the road in a cloud of pink dust, and, rounding a distant turn, disappeared from sight.

CHAPTER XII

It occurred to Gwendolyn that it would be a very good idea to stop turning stones. The first one set bottom-side up had resulted in the arrival of Jane. And whereas the Policeman had appeared when the second was dislodged, here, following the accidental stub of a toe, were these two—the Piper and Thomas.

The Man-Who-Makes-Faces hurried across to her, his expression dubious. "Bitter pill!" he exclaimed, with a sidewise jerk of the ragged hat. "Gall and wormwood!"

"Oh, yes!" For—sure enough!—there *was* an ill-flavored taste on her lips— a taste that made her regret having lost the candy.

Next, the Policeman came *tick-tocking* up. "The scheme was to kidnap you," he declared wrathfully.

"And keep me from finding my fath-er and moth-er," added Gwendolyn. Now she understood why Jane was so pleased with the choice of the automobile road! And she realized that all along there was never any danger of her being kidnaped by *strangers*, but by the two who, their past ill-feeling evidently forgotten, were at this very moment chuckling and chattering together, ugly heads touching—the eary head and the head with the double face!

Seeing the Policeman and the little old gentleman in conversation with Gwendolyn, the Piper slouched over. "Look a-here!" he began roughly, addressing all three; "you're goin' to make a great big mistake if you antagonize a man that belongs to a Labor Union." (Just so had he spoken the day he fixed the broken hot-water pipe.)

"Bosh!" cried the Policeman. "What do we care about *him!* Why, he'll never even get through the Gate!"

Gwendolyn was puzzled. *What* Gate? And *why* would Thomas not get through it? Then looking round to where he was conspiring with Jane, she saw what she believed was a very good explanation: He would never even get through the Gate because (a simple reason!) the *nurse* would not be able to get through.

For by now Jane was not only as *round* as a barrel, but she was fully as *large*—what with so much happy giggling over Thomas's arrival. Moreover, having toppled sidewise, she *looked* like a barrel—a barrel upholstered in black sateen, with a neat touch of white at collar and cuffs!

"He's been in trouble before," continued the Policeman, stormily. "But *this* time—!" And letting himself down flat upon his head, he shook both neatly shod feet in the Piper's face.

It was now that Gwendolyn chanced, for the first time, to examine the latter's bundle. And was surprised to discover that it was nothing less than a large *poke-bonnet*—of the fluffy, lacy, ribbony sort. And she was admiring it, for it was of black silk, and handsome, *when something within it stirred!*

She retreated—until the night-stick and the kidnaper knife were between her and the poke. "Hadn't we better be st-starting?" she faltered nervously.

The Piper marked her manner, and showed instant resentment of it. "This here thing was handed me once in part-payment," he explained. "And I ain't been able to get rid of it since. Every single day it's harder to lug around. Because, you see, he's growin'."

At that, the Policeman and the Man-Who-Makes-Faces exchanged a glance full of significance. And both shrugged—the Policeman with such an emphatic upside-down shrug that his shoulders brushed the ground.

Gwendolyn's curiosity emboldened her. "*He?*" she questioned.

"The pig."

The pig! Gwendolyn's pink mouth opened in amazement. Here was the very pig that she heard *belonged* in a poke!

The Piper was glowering at Jane, who was rocking gently from side to side, displaying first one face, then the other. "Well, *I* call that dancing," he declared. And pulling out a small, well-thumbed account-book, jotted down some figures.

Gwendolyn tried to think of something to say—while feeling mistrust toward the Piper, and abhorrence toward the poke and its contents. At last she took refuge in polite inquiry. "When did you come out from town?" she asked.

The Piper grunted rather ill-humoredly (or was it the pig?—she could not be certain), and colored up a little. "I didn't *come* out," he answered in his surly fashion. Whereupon he fell to fitting a coupling upon the ends of two pipes.

"No?"—inquisitively.

"I—er—got run out."

"Oh!"

Again the Policeman and the Man-Who-Makes-Faces exchanged a significant glance.

"You see," went on the Piper, "in the City everybody's in debt. Well, I have to have my money, don't I? So I dunned 'em all good. But maybe—er—a speck *too* much. So—"

"Oh, dear!" breathed Gwendolyn

"Of course, I've never been what you might call popular. Who *would* be—if everybody owed him money."

"Huh!" snorted the Policeman.

"You overcharge," asserted the little old gentleman.

Gwendolyn hastened to forestall any heated reply from the Piper. "You don't think your pig had anything to do with it?" she suggested considerately. "'Cause do—do *nice* people like pigs?"

"The pig was never in sight," asserted the Piper. "Guess that's one reason why I can't sell him. What people don't see they don't want to buy—even when it's covered up stylish." (Here he regarded the poke with an expression of entire satisfaction.)

The little company was well on its way by now—though Gwendolyn could not recall the moment of starting. The Piper had not waited to be invited, but strolled along with the others, his birch-stemmed tobacco-pipe in a corner of his mouth, his hands in his pockets, and the pig-poke a-swing at his elbow.

Thomas, left to get Jane along as best he could, had managed most ingeniously. The nurse was cylindrical. All he had to do, therefore, was to give her momentum over the smooth windings of the road by an occasional smart shove with both hands.

Which made it clear that the likelihood of losing Jane, of leaving her behind, was lessening with each moment! For now the more the nurse laughed *the easier it would be to get her along.*

"Oh, dear!" sighed Gwendolyn, with a sad shake of her yellow head as Jane came trundling up, both fat arms folded to keep them out of the way.

"If she stopped dancin' where would I come in?" demanded the Piper, resentfully. The pig moved in the poke. He trounced the poor thing irritably.

The Man-Who-Makes-Faces now began to speak—in a curious, chanting fashion. "The mode of locomotion adapted by this woman," said he, "rather adds to, then detracts from, her value as a nurse. Think what facilities she has for amusing a child!—on, say, an extensive slope of lawn. And her ability to, see two ways—practically at once—gives her further value. Would *she* ever let a young charge fall over a cliff?"

The barrel was whopping over and over—noiselessly, except for the faint chatter of Jane's tortoise-shell teeth. Behind it was Thomas, limp-eared by now, and perspiring, but faithful to his task.

"The *best* thing," whispered Gwendolyn, reaching to touch a ragged sleeve, "would be to get rid of Thomas. Then she—"

The Policeman heard. "Get rid of Thomas?" he repeated. "Easy enough. *Look on the ground.*"

She looked.

"See the h's?"

Sure enough, the road was fairly strewn with the sixth consonant!—both in small letters and capitals.

"Been dropped," went on the Officer.

She had heard the expression "dropping his h's." Now she understood it. "Oh, but how'll these help?"

"Show 'em to Thomas!"

She approached the barrel—and pointed down.

Thomas followed her pointing. Instantly his expression became furious. And one by one his ears stood up alertly. "It's him!" he shouted. "Oh, wait till I get my hands on him!" Then heaving hard at the barrel, he raced off along the alphabetical trail.

Gwendolyn was compelled to run to keep up with him. "What's the trouble?" she asked the Man-Who-Makes-Faces.

"A Dictionarial difference," he answered, his dark-skinned face very grave.

"Oh!" (She resolved to hunt Dictionarial up the moment she was back in the school-room.)

Thomas was shouting once more from where he labored in the lead. "I'll murder him!" he threatened. "This time I'll mur-r-der him!"

Murder? That made matters clear! There was only one person against whom Thomas bore such hot ill-will. "It's the King's English," she panted.

"It's the King's English," agreed the Policeman, *tick-tocking* in rapid *tempo*.

She reached again to tug gently at a ragged sleeve. "Do *you* know him?" she asked.

The round black eyes of the little old gentleman shone proudly down at her. "All nice people are well acquainted with the King's English," he declared —which statement she had often heard in the nursery. Now, however, it embarrassed her, for she was compelled to admit to herself that *she* was not acquainted with the King's English—and he a personage of such consequence!

The Piper hurried alongside, all his pipes rattling. "Just where are we goin', anyhow?" he asked petulantly.

"We're going to the Bear's Den," informed the Man-Who-Makes-Faces.

"And here's the Zoo now," announced the Policeman.

It was unmistakably the Zoo. Gwendolyn recognized the main entrance. For above it, in monster letters formed by electric lights, was a sign, bulbous and blinding—

Villa Sites Borax Starch Shirts.

"So *this* is the Gate you meant!" she called to the Policeman.

The Gate was flung invitingly wide Thomas rushed toward it, his fourteen ears flopping horribly.

"And here *he* is!" cried the Policeman. "On guard."

The next moment—"'Alt!" ordered a harsh voice—a voice with an English accent.

There was a flash of scarlet before Gwendolyn's face—of scarlet so vivid that it blinded. She flung up a hand. But she was not frightened. She knew what it was. And rubbed at her eyes hastily to clear them.

He stood in full view.

As far as outward appearance was concerned, he was exactly the looking person she had pictured in her own mind—young and tall and lusty, with a florid countenance and hair as blonde as her own. And he wore the uniform of an English soldier—short coat of scarlet, all gold braid and brass buttons; dark trousers with stripes; and a little round cap with a chin strap.

But he carried no cane. Instead, as he stepped forward, nose up, chin up, eyes very bold, he swung a most amazing weapon. It was as scarlet as his own coat, as long as he was tall, and polished to a high degree. But it was not unbending, like a sword: It was limber to whippiness, so that as he twirled it about his blonde head it snapped and whistled. And Gwendolyn remembered having seen others exactly like it hanging on the bill-board at the Face-Shop. For it was a tongue!

"Aw! Mah word!" exclaimed the King's English, surveying the halted group.

Gwendolyn could not imagine what word he had in mind, but she thought him very fine. With his air of proud self-assurance, and his fine brilliant uniform, he was strikingly like her own red-coated toy! Anxious to make a favorable impression upon him, she smoothed the gingham dress hastily, brushed back straying wisps of yellow, straightened her shoulders, and assumed a cordial expression of countenance.

"How do you do," she said, curtseying.

He saluted. But blocked the way.

"May we go into the Zoo, please?"

His hand jerked down to his side. "One at a time," he answered; "—all but Thomas."

Thomas had come short with the others. Now as Gwendolyn looked at him she saw that he, also, was armed with a tongue—a warped and twisted affair, rough, but thin along its edges.

"If you try to keep me out," he cried, "I certainly *will* murder you!"

At this juncture the Policeman pit-patted forward and took his station at the left of the Gate. Next, the King's English stepped back until he stood at the right. Between them, hand in hand once more, passed Gwendolyn and the Man-Who-Makes-Faces.

The Piper came next. "Call that a' English tongue?" he asked, with an impudent grin at the soldier's shining weapon.

"Yes, sir."

"Pah!"

Now Thomas gave Jane a quick shove forward—but a shove which sent her only as far as the Gate.

The King's English stared down at her. "How are you?" he said coldly.

"I'm awful uncomfortable," was the mournful answer.

"Then take off your stays," he advised. Whereat the polished tongue glanced through the light, caught Jane fairly around the waist, and with a swift recoil brought her to her feet!

And now Gwendolyn, astonished, saw that too much laughter had again remolded that sateen bulk. The nurse had grown woefully heavy about the shoulders—which put a fearful strain on the stitches of her bodice! and gave her the appearance of a gigantic humming-top! As she swayed a moment on her wide-toed shoes—shoes now utterly lacking buttons—the King's English again struck out, caught her, this time, around the neck, and sent her spinning through the Gate!

"*Zing-g-g-g!*" she laughed dizzily—that laugh the high, persistent note of a top!

Thomas attempted to follow. "I just *will* come in," he cried, wielding his warped weapon with a flourish.

"You shall *not!*" To bar the way, the King's English thrust out his polished tongue.

"I *will!*" *Crack! Crack!*

"You won't!" *Crack! Crack!*

The fight was on! For the combatants, tongue's-length from each other, were prowling to and fro menacingly.

"Oh, there's going to be a tongue-lashing," cried Gwendolyn, frightened.

"I'm the King's Hinglish!"—it was the soldier's slogan.

"This is me!" sang Thomas, saucily flicking at a brass button. His face was all cunning.

Then how the tongues popped!

"This is I!" corrected the King's English promptly. But his face got a trifle more florid.

"Steady!" counseled the little old gentleman.

"I'm hall right," the other cried back.

"Oh, Piper!" said Gwendolyn; "which side are *you* on?"

The Piper shifted his tobacco pipe from one corner of his mouth to the other. "I'm for the man that's got the *cash*," he declared.

There was no doubt about Jane's choice. Seeing Thomas's momentary advantage, she came spinning close to the Gate. "Use h-words, Thomas!" she hummed. "Use h-words!"

Thomas acted upon her advice. "Hack and hit and hammer!" he charged. "Haggle and halve and hamper! Halt and hang and harass!"

"'Ack and 'it and 'ammer!" struck back the King's English, beginning to breath hard. "Aggie and 'alve and 'amper! 'Alt and 'ang and 'arass!"

As the tongues met, Gwendolyn saw small bright splinters fly this way and that—a shower of them! These splinters darted downward, falling upon the road. And each, as it lit, was an h!

The Policeman was frightened. "Which is your best foot?" he called.

The King's English indicated his right. "This!"

"Then put it forward!"

"My goodness!" exclaimed Gwendolyn. "Am I seeing this, or is it just Pretend?"

Thomas now warmed to the fray. "Harm!" he scourged, "Harness! Hash! Hew! Hoodwink! Hurt and hurk!"

"'Eavens!" breathed the King's English.

"Turn your cold shoulder," advised the little old gentleman.

The King's English thrust out the right. And it helped! "Oh, hayches don't matter," he panted. "I'm hall right has long has 'is grammar doesn't get too bad." And off came one of Thomas's ears—a large one—and blew along the ground like a great leaf.

That was an unfortunate boast. For Thomas, enraged by the loss of an ear, fought with renewed zeal. "If you see he, just tell I!" he shouted.

The King's English went pallid. "If you see 'im, just tell me," he gasped, meeting Thomas gallantly—with the loss of only one splinter.

"Oh, I want you to win!" called Gwendolyn to him.

But the contest was unequal. That was now plain. The King's English had polish and finish. Thomas had more: his tongue, newly sharpened, cut deep at each blow.

Unequal as was the contest, Jane's interference a second time made it more so. For as the fighters trampled to and fro, seeking the better of each other, she twirled near again. "Try your *verbs*, Thomas!" she counseled. "Try your verbs!"

Eagerly Thomas grasped this second hint. "By which I could was!" he cried, with a curling stroke of the warped tongue; "or shall am!"

At that, the King's English showed distressing weakness. He seemed scarcely to have enough strength for another snap. "By w'ich I could be!" he whipped back feebly; "or shall 'ave been!" And staggered sidewise.

Now the warped and twisted tongue began to chant past-participially: "I done! I done!! I done!!!"

"'Elp!" implored the King's English, fairly wan. "Friends, this—this fellow 'as treated me houtrageously for—for yaaws!"

"Oh, worser and worser and worser," pursued Thomas, changing suddenly to adverbs.

"Rawly now—!" The King's English tottered to his knees.

"I *did*," prompted Gwendolyn, eager to help him.

"I did," repeated the King's English—but the polished tongue slipped from his grasp!

"I seen!" followed up Thomas. "I sung!" *Crack! Crack!*

It was the last fatal onslaught.

The scarlet-coated figure fell forward. Yet bravely he strove again to give tongue-lash for tongue-lash—by reaching out one palsied hand toward his weapon.

"I—I—s-a-w!" he muttered; "I s-s-s-ing!"—And expired, with his last breath gasping good grammar.

Instantly Thomas leaped the prostrate figure and strode to the Gate. He was breathing hard, but looking about him boldly. "Now *I* come through," he boasted.

"O-o-o!" It was Gwendolyn's cry. "Officer, don't let him! *Don't!*"

In answer to her appeal, the Policeman seized Thomas by a lower ear and shoved him against a gate-post. "You've committed murder!" he cried. "And I arrest you!"

"Tongue-tie him!" shouted the little old gentleman, springing to jerk Thomas's weapon out of his hand, and to snatch up the nicked and splintered weapon of the vanquished soldier.

Under the great blazing sign of the Zoo entrance the capture was accomplished. And in a moment, from his feet to his very ears, Thomas was wrapped, arms tight against sides, in the scarlet toils of the tongues.

"So!" exclaimed the little old gentleman as he tied a last knot. "Thomas'll never bother my little girl again." And taking Gwendolyn by the hand, he led her away.

It was not until she had gone some distance that she turned to take a last look back. And saw, there beside the wide Gate, a rubber-plant, its long leaves waving gently. It was Thomas, bound securely, and abandoned.

Yet she did not pity him. He had murdered the King's English, and he deserved his punishment. Furthermore, he looked so green, so cool, so ornamental!

CHAPTER XIII

So far, the Piper had seemed to be no one's friend—unless, perhaps, his own. He had lagged along, surly or boisterous by turns, and careless of his manners; not even showing respect to the Man-Who-Makes-Faces and the Policeman! But now Gwendolyn remarked a change in him. For as he spoke to her, he took his pipe out of his mouth—under the pretext of cleaning it.

"Say!" he began in a cautious undertone: "I'll give you some advice about Jane."

Gwendolyn was looking about her at the Zoo. Its roofs seemed countless. They touched, having no streets between them anywhere, and reached as far as she could see. They were all heights, all shapes, all varieties—some being level, others coming to a point at one corner, a few ending in a tower. One tower, on the outer-most edge of the Zoo, was square, and tapered.

"Jane?" she said indifferently. "Oh, she's only a top."

"Only a top!" It was the little old gentleman. "Why, that makes her all the *more* dangerous!"

"Because she's spinning so fast"—the Policeman balanced on one arm while he shook an emphatic finger—"that she'll stir up trouble!"

"Well, then, what shall I do?" asked Gwendolyn. For, elated over seeing Thomas disposed of so completely—and yet with so much mercy—she was impatient at hearing that she still had reason to fear the nurse.

The Piper took his time about replying. He sharpened one end of a match, thrust the bit of pine into the stem of his pipe, jabbed away industriously, threw away the match, blew through the stem once or twice, and turned the bowl upside down to make it *plop, plop* against a palm. Then, "Keep Jane laughin'," he counseled, "—*and see what happens.*"

Jane was alongside, spinning comfortably on her shoe-leather point. Now, as if she had overheard, or guessed a plot, sudden uneasiness showed on both her countenances, and she increased her speed.

"You done up Thomas, the lot of you," she charged, as she whirled away. "But you don't git *me*."

"And we won't," declared Gwendolyn, "if we don't hurry up and trip her."

"A *good* idear!" chimed in the Piper.

"If we only had some string!" cried the little old gentleman.

"String won't do," said the Policeman. "We need rope."

There was a high wind sweeping the roofs. And as the three began to run about, searching, it fluttered the Policeman's coat-tails, swelled out the Piper's cap, and tugged at the ragged garb of the Man-Who-Makes-Faces.

"Here's a piece of clothes-line!"

The Policeman made the find—catching sight of the line where it dangled from the edge of a roof. The others hastened to join him. And each seized the rope in both hands, the Piper staying at one end of it, the little old gentleman at the opposite, while Gwendolyn and the Policeman posted themselves at proper distances between. Then forward in a row swept all, carrying the rope with them. It was a curious one of its kind—as black as if it had been tarred, thick at the middle, but noticeably thin at one end.

Jane saw their design. "Ba-a-a!" she mocked. "*I'm* not afraid of you! I'm goin' to turn the Big Rock. *Then* you'll see!" And she made straight toward the square tower in the distance.

"*Oh!*" It was the little old gentleman, beard blown sidewise by the wind. "We musn't let her!"

The Piper, in his excitement, jounced the pig so hard that it squealed. "We ought to be able," he panted, "to manage a top."

"Jane!" bellowed the Policeman, galloping hard. "You must *not* injure that shaft!"

Then Gwendolyn realized that the square *tower* toward which the nurse was spinning was the Big Rock. And she recognized it as a certain great pillar of pink granite, up and down the sides of which, deep cut by chisels, were written strange words.

It rose just ahead. Answering the Officer with a shrill, scoffing laugh, Jane bore down upon it. Aided by the wind, she made top speed.

There was not a moment to lose. Her pursuers fairly tore after her. And the Piper, who made the fastest progress, gained—until he was at her very heels. Then with a final leap, he passed her, and circled, dragging the rope.

It made a loop about the buttonless shoes—a loop that tightened as the little old gentleman came short, as the Piper halted. Each gave a pull—

With disastrous result! For as the line came taut, up Jane went!—caught bodily from the ground. And still spinning, whizzed forward in that high wind and struck the granite squarely.

She fell to the ground, toppling sidewise, and bulking large.

But the shaft! It began to move—slowly at first—to tip forward, farther and farther. When, gaining velocity, with a great grinding noise, down from off the massive cube upon which it stood it came crashing!

Instantly a chorus of cries arose: "Oh, she's bumped over the obelisk! She's bumped over the obelisk!"

With the cries, and sounding from beneath the tapered end of the Big Rock, mingled ferocious growls—"*Rar! Rar! Rar! Rar!*"

And in that same moment, the four who were holding the rope felt it begin to writhe and twist in their grasp!—*like a live thing*. And its black length took on a scaly look, glittering in that pink glow as if it were covered with small ebon *paillettes*. It grew cold and clammy. At its thicker end Gwendolyn saw that the Piper was supporting a head—a head with small, fiery eyes and a tongue flame-like in its color and swift darting. Next, "*Hiss-s-s-s-s!*" And with one hideous contortion, the huge black body wrung itself free and coiled.

Once Gwendolyn had boasted that she was not afraid of snakes. And now she did not flee, though the black coils were piled at her very feet. For she recognized the serpent. There was no mistaking that thin face and those small eyes. Moreover, a pocket-handkerchief was bound round the reptilian jaws and tied at the top of the head in a bow-knot.

She had gotten rid of Thomas. But here was Miss Royle!

There was no time for greetings. Again were sounding those furious growls —"*Rar! Rar! Rar!*"

Jane swung round in a half-circle to warn the governess. "It's that Bear!" she hummed. "Can't you drive him away?"

Miss Royle began to uncoil.

The Policeman was *tick-tocking* up and down. "The Den's damaged!" he lamented.

"*Now*, who's goin' to pay?" demanded the Piper.

"I'm afraid the Bear's hurt," declared the Man-Who-Makes-Faces.

In her eagerness to trip Jane, Gwendolyn had utterly forgotten the Bear's Den. Now she saw it—a large cage, light in color, its bars woven closely together. And she saw too—with horror—that what the Policeman said was true: In falling, the Big Rock had broken the cover of the Den. This cover was flopping up and down on its hinges.

"Oh, he's loose!" she gasped.

"*Rar! Rar! Rar-r-r!*"

The Bear himself was knocking the cover into the air. The top of his head could be seen as he hopped about, evidently in pain.

And now an extraordinary thing happened: A black glittering body shot rustling through the grass to the side of the Den. Then up went a scaly head, and forth darted a flaming tongue—driving the Bear back under the cover!

At which the Bear rebelled. For his growls turned into a muffled protest —"Now, you stop, Miss Royle! I *won't* be treated like this! I *won't!*"

Then Gwendolyn understood Jane's hum! And why the governess had obeyed it so swiftly. The light-colored cage with the loose cover was nothing else than the old linen-hamper! As for the Bear—!

Hair flying, cheeks crimson, eyes shining with quick tears of joy, she darted past Jane, leaped the glittering snake-folds before the hamper, and swung the cover up on its hinges.

"Puffy!" she cried. "Oh, Puffy!"

It was indeed Puffy, with his plushy brown head, his bright, shoe-button eyes, his red-tipped, sharply pointed nose, his adorably tiny ears, and deep-cut, tightly shut, determined mouth. It was Puffy, as dear as ever! As old and as squashy!

He stood up in the hamper to look at her, leaning his front paws—in rather a dignified manner—on the broken edge of the basketry. He was breathing hard from his contest, but smiling nevertheless.

"Ah!" said he, affably. "The Poor Little Rich Girl, I see!"

Gwendolyn's first impulse was to take him up in her arms. But his proud air, combined with the fact that he had grown tremendously, caused her to check the impulse.

"How do you do?" she inquired politely.

"I'm pretty shabby, thank you."

"Oh, it's *so* good to hear your voice again!" she exclaimed. "When you left, I didn't have a chance to tell you good-by."

It was then that she noticed a white something fluttering at his breast, just under his left fore-leg. "Excuse me," she said apologetically, "but aren't you losing your pocket handkerchief?"

Sadly he shook his head. "It's my stuffing," he explained. And gently withdrawing his paw from her eager grasp, laid it upon his breast. "You see, the Big Rock—"

The little old gentleman was beside him, examining the wound; muttering to himself.

"Can you mend him?" asked Gwendolyn. "Oh, Puffy!"

The little old gentleman began to empty his pockets of the articles with which he had provided himself—the ear, the handful of hair, the plump cheek. "Ah! Ah!" he breathed as he examined each one; and to and fro wagged the grizzled beard. "I'm afraid—! I must have help. This is a case that will require a specialist."

The tone was so solemn that it frightened her. "Oh, do you mean we need a *Doctor?*"

Puffy was trembling weakly. "I lost some cotton-batting once before," he half-whispered to Gwendolyn. "It was when you were teething. Oh, I know it was unintentional! You were *so* little. But—I can't spare any more."

Down into the patch-pocket went her hand. Out came the lip-case. She thrust it into his furry grasp. "Keep this," she bade, "till I come back. *I'll* go for the Doctor."

The Man-Who-Makes-Faces leaned down. "Fly!" he urged.

At that, Jane began to circle once more. "Lovie," she hummed, "don't you go! He'll give you nasty medicine!"

"Hiss-s-s-s!" chimed in Miss Royle, her bandaged head rising and lowering in assent. "He'll cut out your appendix."

One moment she hesitated, feeling the old fear drive the blood from her cheeks—to her wildly beating heart. Then she saw Puffy sway, half fainting. And obeying the command of the little old gentleman, she grasped her gingham dress at either side—held it out to its fullest width—and with the wind pouching the little skirt, left the high grass, passed up through the lights of the nearby trees—and rose into the higher air!

She gave a glance down as she went. How excitedly Jane was circling! How Miss Royle was lashing the ground!

But the faces of the other three were smiling encouragement. And she flew for her very life. Lightly she went—as if there were nothing to her but her little gingham dress; as if that empty dress, having tugged at some swagging clothes-line until it was free, were now being wafted across the roofs, the tree-tops, the smooth windings of a road, to—

A bake-shop, without doubt! For her nostrils caught the good smell of fresh bread. Suddenly the shop loomed ahead of her. She alighted to have a look at it.

It was a round, high, stone building, with stone steps leading up to it from every side, and columns ranged in a circle at the top of the steps. Seated on the bottom step, engrossed in some task, was a man.

As Gwendolyn looked at him she told herself that the Man-Who-Makes-Faces had given this customer such a nice face; the eyes, in particular, were kind.

He had a large pan of bread-dough beside him. Out of it, now, he gouged a spoonful, which he began to roll between his palms. And as he rolled the dough, it became rounder and rounder, until it was ball-like. It turned browner and browner, too, precisely as if it were baking in his hands! When he was finished with it, he piled it to one side, atop other brown pellets.

She advanced to speak. "Please," she began, pointing a small finger, "what is this place?"

He glanced up. "This, little girl, is the Pillery."

The Pillery! Instantly she knew what he was making—*bread-pills.*

And the bread-pills helped her to recognize him. She dimpled cordially. "I haven't seen you since I had the colic," she said, nodding, "but I know you. You're the Doctor!"

The Doctor was most cordial, shaking her hand gently; after which, naturally enough, he felt her pulse.

"But there's nothing the matter with *me*," she protested. "It's my dear Puffy. *You* remember."

Now he rose solemnly, selected a fresh-baked pill, bowed to the right, again to the left, last of all, to her—and presented the pill.

"In that case, Miss Gwendolyn," he said, smiling down, "a toast!"

And—quite in contrast to the evening of her seventh birthday anniversary—toast there *was*, deliciously crisp and crunchy!

"Oo! How good!" she exclaimed, not nibbling conventionally, but taking big bites. "'Cause I hate cake!"

The next moment she became aware of the munching of others. And on looking round, found that she was back at the Den. She was not surprised. Things had a way of coming to pass in a pleasantly instantaneous fashion. And she was glad to see the little old gentleman, the Piper and the Policeman each fairly gobbling up a pellet. Miss Royle was eating, too, and Jane was stuffing *both* mouths.

But Puffy was having quite different fare. In front of him stood the Doctor, busily feeding filmy white bits into the tear just under a fore-leg.

"I think you'll find," assured the latter, "that a proper amount of cotton-batting is most refreshing."

"Once I wanted Jane to take me to the Doll Hospital," complained Puffy, his shoe-button eyes hard with resentment; "but she said I was only a little beast."

Gwendolyn looked severe. "Jane, you'll be sorry for that," she scolded.

"Ah-*ha!* my dear!" said the Man-Who-Makes-Faces, addressing the nurse, "at last one of your chickens is coming home to roost!"

Gwendolyn glanced up. And, sure enough, a chicken *was* going past—a small blue hen, who looked exceedingly fagged. (This was an occurrence worth noting. How often had she heard the selfsame remark—and never seen as much as a feather!)

Jane also saw the blue hen. And appeared much disconcerted. "I think I'll take forty winks," she hummed; "—twenty for the front face, and twenty for the back." Whereupon she made a few quick revolutions, landing up against the granite base of the obelisk.

The Doctor had been sewing up the tear in Puffy's coat. Now he finished his seam and knotted the thread. "There!" said he, cheerily. "You're as good as new!"

"Thank you," said Puffy. "And I feel so grateful to you, Miss Gwendolyn, that I must repay your kindness. You've always heard a certain statement about Jane, yonder. Well, I'm going to prove that it's *true*."

"What's true?" asked Gwendolyn, puzzled.

He made no answer. But after a short whispered conference with the Policeman, turned his back and began sniffing and snarling under his breath, while a fore-paw was busy in the region of his third rib. When he faced round again, the shoe-button eyes were shining triumphantly, and he was holding both fore-paws together tightly.

"I found one!" he cried. And wabbling over to Jane, stationed himself on one side of her, at the same time motioning the Officer to steal round to the other side on quiet hands.

And now Gwendolyn saw that Jane, though she was only feigning sleep, was ignorant of what was happening. For her double equipment of faces had its disadvantages. Even when upright she had not been able to roll one eye forward while its mate was on guard in the rear. And reclining flat upon her back, she could not rumble her eyes forward to her front face for the reason that they would not roll up-hill. Both stayed in the back of her head, where they could see only the ground.

Very cautiously Puffy put his fore-paws to Jane's ear—suddenly separated them—and waited.

A moment. Then, "Well, finding *this* out, you can wager I don't stay heels over head no more!" cried the Policeman. And with a wriggle and a twist and a bound, he gave a half somersault and stood on his feet!

At once, the bottoms of his trouser-legs came down over his shoes, his coat-tails fell about him properly, uncovering his shield and his belt, and his club took its place at his right side. "Ouch!" he exclaimed. And began to scratch hard at the spot just between his shoulder-blades. At the same time, the tears that were in his cap flowed out and down his face. So that he seemed to be weeping.

The Doctor, leaning close beside Gwendolyn, was all sympathy. "There is no reason to feel bad," he said kindly. "The operation was successful."

"Feel bad!" repeated the Policeman. "Why, I'm *laughing*. Ha! Ha! We put a flea in her ear!"

At that, Jane began to laugh "Oh, laws!" she exclaimed, sleeve to mouth once more. "Oh, I never heard the like of it!"

"*Rar!*" growled Puffy, delighted. "The plan is working! See her growl!"

"That flea went in one ear and came out the other," declared the little old gentleman, poking Jane with the toe of a worn shoe.

Jane laughed the harder. "Oh, it's awful funny!" she cried, rocking herself to and fro—and steadily increasing her girth. "Oh! Oh! Oh!"

"We've proved that you're empty-headed," said Puffy.

And now the nurse was seized by a very paroxysm of mirth. Both faces distorted, she whopped over and over.

"That's right! Split your sides alaughin'," cried the Piper.

At these words, sudden terror showed on her face. For the first time she saw the trap into which she had been led!

Yet she could not check her laughter. "Oh, ho!" she gasped hysterically; "*oh!—*"

It was her last. Black sateen could stand no more.

She gave a final and feeble rock. Both revolving faces paled. Then there sounded a loud *pop*—like the bursting of an automobile tire. Next, a ripping—

"Look!" cried Gwendolyn.

There were great rents down the front seams of Jane's waist!

The nurse guessed what had happened, and clutched desperately at the gaping seams with both fat hands—now in front, now at the sides, striving to hold the rips together.

To no avail! All the laughter was gone out of her. Quickly she collapsed, her sateen hanging in loose, ragged strips. Once more she was just ordinary nurse-maid size.

"Oh, will she die?" asked Gwendolyn, anxiously.

The Doctor knelt to grasp Jane's wrist. "No," he answered gravely; "she'll only have to go back to the Employment Agency."

"I won't!" cried Jane. "*I* won't!—Miss Royle!"

"*Hiss-ss-ss!*"

"Get you-know-what out of the way! A certain person musn't talk to it! If she does she'll find—"

"I understand!" hissed back the snake.

You-know-what? Gwendolyn was troubled.

Now the Policeman and the Piper, assisted by Puffy, picked the nurse up and packed her into the linen-hamper. Whereupon the little old gentleman slapped down the cover and tied a large tag to it. On the tag was written— *Employment Agency, Down-Town!*"

"I'm done with *her*" said Gwendolyn; "—if she *is* a perfectly good top."

"You're rid of me," answered Jane, calling through the weave of the hamper "*Yes!* But how about *Miss Royle?*"

"We'll send her back too," declared the Man-Who-Makes-Faces. "Here! Where *are* you?" He ran about, searching.

The others searched also—through the grass, behind the granite shift, everywhere. Concern sobered each face.

For the snake-in-the-grass was gone!

CHAPTER XIV

Why had Miss Royle, sly reptile that she was, scuttled away without so much as a good-by?

"Oh, dear!" sighed Gwendolyn; "just as soon as one trouble's finished, another one starts!"

"We must get on her track!" declared the Policeman, patroling to and fro anxiously.

"And let's hurry," urged the Man-Who-Makes-Faces. "It's coming night in the City. And all these lights'll be needed soon."

Very soon, indeed. For even as he spoke it happened—with a sharp click. Instantly the pink glow was blotted out. As suddenly thick blackness shut down.

Except straight ahead! There Gwendolyn made out an oblong patch of sky in which were a few dim stars.

"Never mind," went on the little old gentleman, soothingly. "Because we're close to the place where there's light all the time."

"*All* the time?" repeated Gwendolyn, surprised.

"It's where light grows."

"*Grows?*"

"Well, it's where *candle*-light grows."

"Candle-light!" she cried. "You mean—! Oh, it's where my fath-er comes!"

"Sometimes."

"Will he be there now?"

"Only the Bird can tell us that."

Then she understood Jane's last gasping admonition—"Get you-know-what out of the way! A certain person mustn't talk to it! If she does she'll find—"

It was the Doctor's hand that steadied her as she hurried forward in the darkness. It was a big hand, and she was able to grasp only two fingers of it. But that clinging hold made her feel that their friendship was established. She was not at all surprised at her complete change of attitude toward him. It seemed to her now as if he and she had always been on good terms.

The others were near. She could hear the *tinkle-tankle* of the Piper's pipes, the scuff of Puffy's paws, the labored breathing of the little old gentleman as he trudged, the heavy tramp, tramp of the Policeman. She made her bare feet travel as fast as she could, and kept her look steadily ahead on the dim stars.

And saw, moving from one to another of them, in quick darts—now up, now down—a small Something. She did not instantly guess what it was— flitting across that half-darkened sky. Until she heard the wild beating of tiny pinions!

"Why, it's a bird!" she exclaimed.

"A bird?" repeated the Policeman, all eagerness.

"Must be *the* Bird!" declared the Man-Who-Makes-Faces, triumphantly.

It was. Even in the poor light her eager eyes made out the bumps on that small feathered head. And saw that on the down-drooping tail, nicely balanced, and gleaming whitely, was a lump.

Remembering what she had heard about that bit of salt, she ran forward. At her approach, his wings half-lifted. And as she reached out to him, pointing a small finger, he sprang sidewise, alighting upon it.

"Oh, I'm glad you've come!" he panted.

He was no larger than a canary; and seemed to be brown—a sparrow- brown. Prejudiced against him she had been. He had tattled about her— *worse,* about her father. Yet seeing him now, so tiny and ruffled and frightened, she liked him.

She brought him to a level with her eyes. "What's the matter?" she asked soothingly.

"I'm afraid." He thrust out his head, pointing. "*Look*."

She looked. Ahead the tops of the grass blades were swaying this way and that in a winding path—as if from the passage of some crawling thing!

"She tried to get me out of the way!"

"Oh, tell me where is my fath-er!"

"Why, of *course*. They say he's—"

He did not finish; or if he did she heard no end to the sentence. Of a sudden her face had grown almost painfully hot—as a great yellow light flamed against it, a light that shimmered up dazzlingly from the surface of a broad treeless field. This field was like none that she had ever imagined. For its acres were neatly sodded with *mirrors*.

The little company was on the beveled edge of the field. To halt them, and conspicuously displayed, was a sign. It read—

"'Keep off the glass,'" read Gwendolyn. "And I don't wonder. 'Cause we'd crack it."

"We don't crack it, we cross it," reminded the Man-Who-Makes-Faces. And stepped boldly upon the gleaming plate.

"My! My!" exclaimed the Piper. "Ain't there a *fine* crop this year!"

A fine crop? Gwendolyn glanced down. And saw for the first time that the mirrored acres were studded, flower-like, with countless silk-shaded candles!

What curious candles they were! They did not grow horizontally, as she had imagined they must, but upright and candle-like. Above their sticks, which were of brass, silver and decorated porcelain, was a flame, ruddy of tip, sharply pointed, but fat and yellow at the base, where the soft white wax fed the fire; at the other end of the sticks, as like the top light as if it were a perfect reflection, was a second flame. These were candles that burned *at both ends*.

And this was the region she had traveled so far to find! Her heart beat so wildly that it stirred the plaid of the little gingham dress.

"Say! I hear a quacking!" announced Puffy, staring up into the sky.

Gwendolyn heard it, too. It seemed to come from across the Field of Double-Ended Candles. She peered that way, to where a heavy fringe of trees walled the farther side greenily.

She saw him first!—while the others (excepting the Bird) were still staring skyward. At the start, what she discerned was only a faint outline on the tree-wall—the outline of a man, broad-shouldered, tall, but a trifle stooped. It was faint for the reason that it blended with the trees. For the man was garbed in green.

As he advanced into the field, the chorus of quacks grew louder. And presently Gwendolyn caught certain familiar expressions—"Oh, don't bozzer me!" "Sit up straight, Miss! Sit up straight!" (this a rather deep quack). "My dear child, you have no sense of time!" And, "What on earth ever put such a question into your head!" She concluded that the expressions were issuing from the large bell-shaped horn which was pointed her way over one shoulder of the man in green. The talking-machine to which the horn was attached—a handsome mahogany affair—he carried on his back. It was not unlike a hand-organ. Which made Gwendolyn wonder if he was not the Man-Who-Makes-Faces' brother.

She glanced back inquiringly at the little old gentleman. Either the stranger *was* a relation—and not a popular one—or else the quacking expressions annoyed. For the Man-Who-Makes-Faces was scowling. And, "Cavil, criticism, correction!" he scolded, half to himself.

He in green now began to move about and gather silk-shaded candles, bending this way and that to pluck them, and paying not the slightest attention to the group of watchers in plain view. But not one of these was indifferent to *his* presence. And all were acting in a most incomprehensible manner. With one accord, Doctor and Piper, Bear and Policeman, Face-maker and Bird, were rubbing hard at the palm of one hand. There being no trees close by, the men used the sole of a shoe, while Puffy raked away at one paw with the claws of the others, and the Bird pecked a foot with his beak.

And yet Gwendolyn could not believe that it was really *he*.

The Policeman drew near. "You've heard of Hobson's choice?" he inquired in a low voice. "Perhaps this is Hobson, or Sam Hill, or Punch, or Great Scott."

The Man-Who-Makes-Faces shook his head. "You don't know him," he answered, "because recently, when the bears were bothering him a lot in his Street, I made him a long face."

The man in green was pausing where the candles clustered thickest. Gwendolyn, still doubtful, went forward to greet him.

"How do you do, sir," she began, curtseying.

His face was long, as the Man-Who-Makes-Faces had pointed out—very long, and pale, and haggard. Between his sunken temples burned his dark-rimmed eyes. His nose was thin, and over it the skin was drawn so tightly that his nostrils were pinched. His lips were pressed together, driving out the blood. His cheeks were hollow, and shadowed bluely by a day-old beard. He had on a hat. Yet she was able (curiously enough!) to note that his hair was sparse over the top of his head, and streaked with gray.

Nevertheless there was no denying that she recognized him dimly.

Something knotted in her throat—at seeing weariness, anxiety, even torture, in those deep-set eyes. "I think I've met you before somewhere," she faltered. "Your—your long face—" The Bird was perched on the fore-finger of one hand. She proffered the other.

He did not even look at her. "My hands are full," he declared. And again, "My hands are full."

She glanced at them. And saw that each was indeed full—of paper money. Moreover, the green of his coat was the green of new crisp bills. While his buff-colored trousers were made of yellowish ones, carefully creased.

He was literally *made of money*.

Now she felt reasonably certain of his identity. Yet she determined to make even more sure. "Would you mind just turning around for a moment?" she inquired.

"But I'm busy to-day," he protested, "I can't be bothered with little girls. I'll see you when you're eight years old." Nevertheless he faced about accommodatingly.

The moment he turned his back he displayed a detail of his dress that had not been visible before. This detail, at first glance, appeared to be a smart leather piping. On second glance it seemed a sort of shawl-strap contrivance by which the talking-machine was suspended. But in the end she knew what it was—a leather harness!—an exceedingly handsome, silver-buckled, hand-sewed harness!

She went around him and raised a smiling face—caught at a hand, too; and felt her own happy tears make cool streaks down her cheeks. "I—I don't see you often," she said, "bu-but I know you just the same. You're—you're my fath-er!"

At that, he glanced down at her—stooped—picked a candle—and held it close to her face.

"Poor little girl!" he said. "Poor little girl!"

"Poor little *rich* girl," she prompted, noting that he had left out the word.

She heard a sob!

The next moment, *Rustle! Rustle! Rustle!* And at her feet the gay-topped candles were bent this way and that—as Miss Royle, with an artful serpent-smile on her bandaged face, writhed her way swiftly between them!

"Dearie," she hissed, making an affectionate half-coil about Gwendolyn, "what *do* you think I'm going to say to you!"

Gwendolyn only shook her head.

"*Guess*, darling," encouraged the governess, coiling herself a little closer.

"Maybe you're going to say, 'Use your dictionary,'" ventured Gwendolyn.

"Oh, dearie!" chided Miss Royle, managing a very good blush for a snake.

But now Gwendolyn guessed the reason for the other's sudden display of affection. For that scaly head was rising out of the grass, inch by inch, and those glittering serpent eyes were fixed upon the Bird!

Unable to move, he watched her, plumage on end, round eyes fairly starting.

"*Cheep! Cheep!*"

At his cry of terror, the Doctor interposed. "I think we'd better take the Bird out of here," he said. "The less noise the better." And with that, he lifted the small frightened thing from Gwendolyn's finger.

Miss Royle, quite thrown off her poise, sank hissing to the ground. "My neuralgia's worse than ever this evening," she complained, affecting not to notice his interference.

"Huh!" he grunted. "Keep away from bargain counters."

The Piper came jangling up. "That snake belongs in her case," he declared, addressing the Doctor.

More than once Gwendolyn had wondered why the Piper had burdened himself—to all appearances uselessly and foolishly—with the various pieces of lead pipe. But now what wily forethought she granted him. For with a few quick flourishes of the wrench, she saw him join them, end to end, to form one length. This he threw to the ground, after which he gave a short, sharp whistle.

In answer to it, the Bird fluttered down, and entered one end of the pipe, giving, as he disappeared from sight, one faint cheep.

Miss Royle heard. Her scaly head glittered up once more. Her beady eyes shone. Her tongue darted hate. Then little by little, that long black body began to move—toward the pipe!

A moment, and she entered it; another, and the last foot of rustling serpent had disappeared. Then out of the farther end of the pipe bounced the Bird. Whereat the Piper sprang to the Bird's side, produced a nut, and screwed it on the pipe-end.

"How's that!" he cried triumphantly.

The pipe rolled partly over. A muffled voice came from it, railing at him: "Be careful what you do, young man! *I* saw you had that bonnet of mine!"

"Oh, can a snake crawl backwards?" demanded Gwendolyn, excitedly.

The Piper answered with a harsh laugh. And scrambling the length of the lead pipe, fell to hammering in a plug.

Miss Royle was a prisoner!

The Bird bounced very high. "That's a feather in *your* cap," he declared joyously, advancing to the Piper. And suiting the action to the word, pulled a tiny plume from his own wing, fluttered up, and thrust it under the band of the other's greasy head-gear.

"Think how that governess has treated me," growled Puffy. "When I was in your nursery, and was old and a little worn out, *how* I would've appreciated care—and repair!"

"The Employment Agency for her," said the Piper.

"I'll attend to that," added the Policeman.

Gwendolyn's father had been gathering candles, and had seemed not to see what was transpiring. Now as if he was satisfied with his load, he suddenly started away in the direction he had come. His firm stride jolted the talking-machine not a little. The quacking cries recommenced—

"Please to pay me.... Let me sell you...! Let me borrow...! Won't you hire...! *Quack! Quack! Quack!*"

After him hurried the others in an excited group. The Piper led it, his plumbing-tools jangling, his pig-poke a-swing. And Gwendolyn saw him grin back over a shoulder craftily—then lay hold of her father and *tighten a strap*.

She trudged in the rear. She had found her father—and he could see only the candles he sought, and the money in his grasp! She was out in the open with him once more, where she was free to gambol and shout—yet he was bound by his harness and heavily laden.

"I might just as well be home," she said to Puffy, disheartened.

"Wish your father'd let me sharpen his ears," whispered the Man-Who-Makes-Faces. He shifted the hand-organ to the other shoulder.

The Doctor had a basket on his arm. He peered into it. "I haven't a thing about me," he declared, "but a bread-pill."

"How would a glass of soda-water do?" suggested the Policeman, in an undertone.

"Why, of *course!*"

It had happened before that the mere mention of a thing brought that dying swiftly. Now it happened again. For immediately Gwendolyn heard the rush and bubble and brawl of a narrow mountain-stream. Next, looking down from the summit of a gentle rise, she saw the smoky windings of the unbottled soda!

The Doctor was a man of action. Though the Policeman had made his suggestion only a second before, here was the former already leaning down to the stream; and, having dipped, was walking in the midst of the little company, glass in hand.

Gwendolyn ran forward. "Fath-er!" she called; "*please* have a drink!"

Her father shook his head. "I'm not thirsty," he declared, utterly ignoring the proffered glass.

"I—I was 'fraid he wouldn't," sighed Gwendolyn, head down again, and scuffing bare feet in the cool damp grass of the stream-side—yet not enjoying it! The lights had changed: The double-ended candles had disappeared. Filling the Land once more with a golden glow were countless tapers—electric, gas, and kerosene. She was back where she had started, threading the trees among which she had danced with joy.

But she was far from dancing now!

"Let's not give up hope," said a voice—the Doctor's. He was holding up the glass before his face to watch the bubbles creaming upon its surface. "There may be a sudden turn for the better."

Before she could draw another breath—here was the turn! a sharp one. And she, felt a keen wind in her eyes,—blown in gusts, as if by the wings of giant butterflies. The cloud that held the wind lay just ahead—a pinky mass that stretched from sky to earth.

The Bird turned his dark eyes upon Gwendolyn from where he sat, high and safe, on the Doctor's shoulder. "I think her little journey's almost done," he said. There was a rich canary note in his voice.

"Oo! goody!" she cried.

"You mean you have a solution?" asked the little old gentleman.

"A solution?" called back the Piper. "Well—?"

A moment's perfect stillness. Then, "It's simple," said the Bird. (Now his voice was strangely like the Doctor's.) "I suppose you might call it a salt solution."

His last three words began to run through Gwendolyn's mind—"A salt solution! A salt solution! A salt solution!"—as regularly as the pulse that throbbed in her throat.

"Yes,"—the Doctor's voice now, breathless, low, tremulous with anxiety. "If we want to save her—"

"Am I *her?*" interrupted Gwendolyn. (And again somebody sobbed!)

"—*It must be done!*"

"There isn't anything to cry about," declared Gwendolyn, stoutly. She felt hopeful, even buoyant.

It was all novel and interesting. The Doctor began by making grabs at the lump of salt on the Bird's tail. The lump loosened suddenly. He caught it between his palms, after which he began to roll it—precisely as he had rolled the dough at the Pillery. And as the salt worked into a more perfect ball, it slowly browned!

Gwendolyn clapped her hands. "My father won't know the difference," she cried.

"You get my idea exactly," answered the Bird.

The Doctor uncovered the pill-basket, selected a fine, round, toasted example of his own baking, and presented it to the Man-Who-Makes-Faces; presented a second to Gwendolyn; thence went from one to another of the little company, whereat everyone fell to eating.

At once Gwendolyn's father looked round the circle of picknickers—as if annoyed by the crunching; but when the Doctor held out the brown salt, he took it, examined it critically, turning it over and over, then lifted it—and bit.

"Pretty slim lunch this," he observed.

He ate heartily, until the last salt crumb was gone. Then, "I'm thirsty," he declared "Where's—?"

Instantly the Doctor proffered the glass. And the other drank—in one great gasping mouthful.

"Ah!" breathed Gwendolyn. And felt a grateful coolness on her lips, as if she had slaked her own thirst.

The next moment her father turned. And she saw that the change had already come. First of all, he looked down at his hands, caught sight of the crumpled bills, and attempted to stuff them hurriedly into his pocket. But his pockets were already wedged tight with silk-shaded candles. He reached round and fed the bills into the mahogany case of the talking-machine. Next, he emptied his pockets of the double-ended candles, frowned at them, and threw them to one side to wilt. Last of all, he spied a bit of leather strap, and pulled at it impatiently. Whereupon, with a clear ring of its silver mountings, his harness fell about his feet.

He smiled, and stepped out of it, as out of a cast-off garment. This quick movement shook up the talking-machine, and at once voices issued from the great horn shrilly protesting into his ear—"*Quack!* Quack! *Kommt, Fraulein!*" "*Une fille stupider!*" "*Gid-dap!*" "*Honk! Honk! Honk!*"—and then, rippling upward, to the accompaniment of dancing feet, a scale on a piano.

He peered into the horn. "When did I come by *this?*" he demanded. "Well, I shan't carry it another step!" And moving his shoulders as if they ached, let the talking-machine slip sidewise to the glass.

There was a crank attached to one side of the machine. This he grasped. And while he continued to stuff bills into the mahogany box with one hand, he turned the crank with the other. Gwendolyn had often marveled at the way bands of music, voices of men and women, chimes of clocks, and bugle-calls could come out of the self-same place. Now this was made clear to her. For as her father whirled the crank, out of the horn, in a little procession, waddled the creatures who had quacked so persistently.

There were six of them in all. One wore patent leather pumps; one had a riding-whip; the third was in motor-livery—buff and blue; another waddled with an air unmistakably French (feathers formed a boa about her neck); the next advanced firmly, a metronome swinging on a slender pince-nez chain; the last one of all carried a German dictionary.

Her father observed them gloomily. "*That's* the kind of ducks and drakes I've been making out of my money," he declared.

The procession quacked loudly, as if glad to get out. And waddled toward the stream.

"Why!" cried Gwendolyn; "there's Monsieur Tellegen, and my riding-master, and the chauffeur, and my French teacher, and my music-teacher, and my Ger—!"

His eyes rested upon her then. And she saw that he knew her!

"Oh, daddy!"—the tender name she loved to call him.

"Little daughter! Little daughter!"

She felt his arms about her, pressing her to him. His pale face was close. "When my precious baby is strong enough—," he began.

"I'm strong *now*." She gripped his fingers.

"We'll take a little jaunt together."

"We must have moth-er with us, daddy. Oh, *dear* daddy!"

"We'll see mother soon," he said; "—*very* soon."

She brushed his cheek with searching fingers. "I think we'd better start right away," she declared. "'Cause—isn't this a rain-drop on your face?"

CHAPTER XV

Without another moment's delay Gwendolyn and her father set forth, traveling a road that stretched forward beside the stream of soda, winding as the stream wound, to the music of the fuming water—music with a bass of deep pool-notes.

How sweet it all was! Underfoot the dirt was cool. It yielded itself deliciously to Gwendolyn's bare tread. Overhead, shading the way, were green boughs, close-laced, but permitting glimpses of blue. Upon this arbor, bouncing along with an occasional chirp of contentment, and with the air of one who has assumed the lead, went the Bird.

Gwendolyn's father walked in silence, his look fixed far ahead. Trotting at his side, she glanced up at him now and then. She did not have to dread the coming of Jane, or Miss Royle, or Thomas. Yet she felt concern—on the score of keeping beside him; of having ready a remark, gay or entertaining, should he show signs of being bored.

No sooner did the thought occur to her than the Bird was ready with a story. He fluttered down to the road, hunted a small brush from under his left wing and scrubbed carefully at the feathers covering his crop. "Now I can make a clean breast of it," he announced.

"Oh, you're going to tell us how you got the lump?" asked Gwendolyn, eagerly.

The feathers over his crop were spotless. He nodded—and tucked away the scrubbing brush. "Once upon a time," he began—

She dimpled with pleasure. "I like stories that start that way!" she interrupted.

"Once upon a time," he repeated, "I was just an ordinary sparrow, hopping about under the kitchen-window of a residence, busily picking up crumbs. While I was thus employed, the cook in the kitchen happened to spill some salt on the floor. Being a superstitious creature she promptly threw a lump of it over her shoulder. Well, the kitchen window was open, and the salt went through it and lit on my tail," (Here he pointed his beak to where the crystal had been). "And no sooner did it get firmly settled on my feathers —"

"The first person that came along could catch you!" cried Gwendolyn, "Jane told me *that*."

"Jane?" said the Bird.

"The fat two-faced woman that was my nurse."

The Bird ruffled his plumage. "Well, of course she knew the facts," he admitted "You see, *she was the cook*."

"Oh!"

"As long as that lump was on my tail," resumed the Bird, "anybody could catch me, and send me anywhere. And nobody ever seemed to want to take the horrid load off—with salt so cheap."

"Did you do errands for my fath-er?"

Her father answered. "Messages and messages and messages," he murmured wearily. (There was a rustle, as of paper.) "Mostly financial," He sighed.

"Sometimes my work has eased up a trifle," went on the Bird, more cheerily; "that's when They hired Jack Robinson, because he's so quick."

"Oh, yes, you worked for They," said Gwendolyn. "Please, who are They? And what do They look like? And how many are there of 'em?"

Ahead was a bend in the road. He pointed it out with his bill. "You know," said he, "it's just as good to turn a corner as a stone. For there They are now!" He gave an important bounce.

She rounded the bend on tiptoe. But when she caught sight of They, it seemed as if she had seen them many times before. They were two in number, and wore top hats, and plum-covered coats with black piping. They were standing in the middle of the road, facing each other. About their feet fluttered dingy feathers. And between them was a half-plucked crow, which They were picking.

Once she had wanted to thank They for the pocket in the new dress. Now she felt as if it would be ridiculous to mention patch-pockets to such stately personages. So, leaving her father, she advanced modestly and curtsied.

"How do you do, They," she began. "I'm glad to meet you."

They stared at her without replying. They were alike in face as well as in dress; even in their haughty expression of countenance.

"I've heard about you so often," went on Gwendolyn. "I feel I almost know you. And I've heard lots of things that you've said. Aren't you always saying things?"

"Saying things," They repeated. (She was astonished to find that They spoke in chorus!) "Well, it's often So-and-So that does the talking, but we get the blame." Now They glared.

Gwendolyn, realizing that she had been unfortunate in the choice of a subject, hastened to reassure them. "Oh, I don't want to blame you," she protested, "for things you don't do."

At that They smiled. "I blame him, and he blames me," They answered. "In that way we shift the responsibility." (At which Gwendolyn nodded understandingly.) "And since we always hunt as a couple" (here They pulled fiercely at the feathers of the captured bird between them) "nobody ever knows who really *is* to blame."

They cast aside the crow, then, and led the way along the road, walking briskly. Behind them walked the Policeman, one hand to his cap.

"Say, please don't put me off the Force," he begged.

Grass and flowers grew along the center of the road. No sooner did the Policeman make his request than They moved across this tiny hedge and traveled one side of the road, giving the other side over to the Officer. Whereupon he strode abreast of They, swinging his night-stick thoughtfully.

The walking was pleasant there by the stream-side. The fresh breeze caressed Gwendolyn's cheeks, and swirled her yellow hair about her shoulders. She took deep breaths, through nostrils swelled to their widest.

"Oh, I like this place best in the whole, whole world!" she said earnestly.

The next moment she knew why! For rounding another bend, she caught sight of a small boyish figure in a plaid gingham waist and jeans overalls. His tousled head was raised eagerly. His blue eyes shone.

"*Hoo*-hoo-oo-oo!" he called.

She gave a leap forward. "Why, it's Johnnie Blake!" she cried. "Johnnie! Oh, Johnnie!"

It was Johnnie. There was no mistaking that small freckled nose. "Say! Don't you want to help dig worms?" he invited. And proffered his drinking-cup.

She needed no urging, but began to dig at once; and found bait in abundance, so that the cup was quickly filled, and she was compelled to use his ragged straw hat. "Oh, isn't this nice!" she exclaimed. "And after we fish let's hunt a frog!"

"I know where there's tadpoles," boasted he. "And long-legged bugs that can walk on the water, and—"

"Oh, I want to stay here always!"

She had forgotten that there were others about. But now a voice—her father's— broke in upon her happy chatter:

"Without your *mother?*"

She had been sitting down. She rose, and brushed her hands on the skirt of her dress. "I'll find my moth-er," she said.

The little old gentleman was beside Johnnie, patting his shoulder and thrusting something into a riveted pocket. "There!" he half-whispered. "And tell your father to be sure to keep this nose away from the grindstone."

Gwendolyn wrinkled her brows. "But—but isn't Johnnie coming with *me?*" she asked.

At that Johnnie shook his head vigorously. "Not away from *here,*" he declared. "No!"

"No," repeated Puffy. "Not away from the woods and the stream and fishing, and hunting frogs and tadpoles and water-bugs. Why, he's the Rich Little Poor Boy!"

"Oh!—Well, then I'll come back!" She moved away slowly, looking over a shoulder at him as she went. "Don't forget! I'll come back!"

"I'll be here," he answered. "And I'll let you use my willow fish-pole." He waved a hand.

There were carriage-lamps along the stream now. Alternating with these were automobile lights—brass side-lights, and larger brass search-lights, all like great glowing eyes.

Again They were in advance. "We can't be very far from the Barn," They announced. And each waved his right arm in a half-circle.

"Robin Hood's Barn?" whispered Gwendolyn.

The Policeman nodded. "The first people to go around it," said he, "were ladies who used feather-dusters on the parlor furniture."

"I s'pose it's been built a long time," said Gwendolyn.

"Ah, a *long* time!" Her father was speaking. Now he halted and pointed down—to a wide road that crossed the one she was traveling. "Just notice how *that's* been worn."

The wide road had deep ruts. Also, here and there upon it were great, bowl-like holes. But a level strip between the ruts and the holes shone as if it had been tramped down by countless feet.

"Around Robin Hood's Barn!" went on her father sadly. "How many have helped to wear that road! Not only her mother, but *her* mother before her, and then back and back as far as you can count."

"I can't count back very far," said Gwendolyn, "'cause I never have any time for 'rithmatic. I have to study my French, and my German, and my music, and my—"

Her father groaned. "I've traveled it, too," he admitted.

She lifted her eyes then. And there, just across that wide road, was the Barn!—looming up darkly, a great framework of steel girders, all bolted together, and rusted in patches and streaks. Through these girders could be seen small regular spots of light.

"Nobody *has* to go round the Barn," she protested. "Anybody could just go right in at one side and right out at the other."

"But the *road!*" said her father meaningly. "If ever one's feet touch it—!"

She thought the road wonderful. It was river-wide, and full of gentle undulations. Where it was smoothest, it reflected the Barn and all the surrounding lights. Yet now (like the shining tin of a roof-top) it resounded —to a foot-fall!

"Some one's coming!" announced the Piper.

Buzz-z-z-z!

It was a low, angry droning.

The next moment a figure came into sight at a corner of the Barn. It was a slender, girlish figure, and it came hurrying forward along the circular way with never a glance to right or left. Gwendolyn could see that whoever the traveler was, her dress was plain and scant. Nor were there ornaments shining in her pretty hair, which was unbound. She was shod in dainty, high-heeled slippers. And now she walked as fast as she could; again she broke into a run; but taking no note of the ruts and rough places, continually stumbled.

"She's watching what's in her hand," said the Man-Who-Makes-Faces. "Contemplation, speculation, perlustration." And he sighed.

"She'll have a fine account to settle with me,"—this the Piper again. He whipped out his note-book. "That's what *I* call a merry dance."

"See what she's carrying," advised the Bird. In one hand the figure held a small dark something.

Gwendolyn looked. "Why,—why," she began hesitatingly, "isn't it a *bonnet?*"

A bonnet it was—a plain, cheap-looking piece of millinery.

BUZZ-Z-Z-Z-Z!

The drone grew loud. The figure caught the bonnet close to her face and held it there, turning it about anxiously. Her eyes were eager. Her lips wore a proud smile.

It was then that Gwendolyn recognized her. And leaned forward, holding out her arms. "Moth-er!" she plead. "*Mother!*"

Her mother did not hear. Or, if she heard, did not so much as lift her eyes from the bonnet. She tripped, regained her balance, and rushed past, hair wind-tossed, dress fluttering. At either side of her, smoke curled away like silk veiling blown out by the swift pace.

"Oh, she's burning!" cried Gwendolyn, in a panic of sudden distress.

The Doctor bent down. "That's money," he explained; "—burning her pockets."

"She can't see anything but the bee. She can't hear anything but the bee." It was Gwendolyn's father, murmuring to himself.

"*The bee!*"

Now the Bird came bouncing to Gwendolyn's side. "You've read that bees are busy little things, haven't you?" he asked. "Well, this particular so-cial hon-ey-gath-er-ing in-sect—"

"That's the very one!" she declared excitedly.

"—Is no exception."

"We must get it away from her," declared Gwendolyn. "Oh, how *tired* her poor feet must be!" (As she said it, she was conscious of the burning ache of her own feet; and yet the tears that swam in her eyes were tears of sympathy, not of pain.) "Puffy! Won't you eat it?"

Puffy blinked as if embarrassed. "Well, you see, a bee—er—makes honey," he began lamely.

The figure had turned a corner of the Barn. Now, on the farther side of the great structure, it was flitting past the openings.

Gwendolyn rested a hand on the wing of the Bird. "Won't *you* eat it?" she questioned.

The Bird wagged his bumpy head. "It's against all the laws of this Land," he declared.

"But this is a *society* bee."

"A bird isn't even allowed to eat a bad bee. But"—chirping low—"I'll tell you what *can* be tried."

"Yes?"

"Ask your mother to trade her bonnet for the Piper's poke."

Gwendolyn stared at him for a moment. Then she understood. "The poke's prettier," she declared. "Oh, if she only would! Piper!"

The Piper swaggered up. "Some collecting on hand?" he asked. Swinging as usual from a shoulder was the poke.

Gwendolyn thought she had never seen a prettier one. Its ribbon bows were fresh and smart; its lace was snow-white and neatly frilled.

"Oh, I *know* she'll make the trade!" she exclaimed happily.

The Piper considered the matter, pursing his lips around the pipe-stem in his mouth; standing on one foot.

Gwendolyn appealed to the Man-Who-Makes-Faces. "Maybe moth-er'll have to have her ears sharpened," she suggested.

The little old gentleman shook his shaggy head. "*Don't let her hear that pig!*" he warned darkly.

"She'll come round in another moment!" It was the Doctor, voice very cheery.

At that, the Piper unslung the poke and advanced to the edge of the road. "I've never wanted this crazy poke," he asserted over a shoulder to Gwendolyn. "Now, I'll just get rid of it. And I'll present that bonnet with the bee" (here he laughed harshly) "to a woman that hasn't footed a single one of my bills. Ha! ha!"

Buzz-z-z-z!

Again that high, strident note. Gwendolyn's mother was circling into sight once more. Fortunately, she was keeping close to the outer edge of the road. The Piper faced in the direction she was speeding, and prepared to race beside her.

BUZZ-Z-Z-Z!

It was an exciting moment! She was holding out the bonnet as before. He thrust the poke between her face and it, carefully keeping the lace and the bows in front of her very eyes.

"Madam!" he shouted. "Trade!"

"Moth-er!"

Her mother heard. Her look fell upon the poke. She slowed to a walk.

"*Trade!*" shouted the Piper again, dangling the poke temptingly.

She stopped short, gazing hard at the poke. "Trade?" she repeated coldly. (Her voice sounded as if from a great distance.) "Trade? Well, that depends upon what They say."

Then she circled on—at such a terrible rate that the Piper could not keep pace. He ceased running and fell behind, breathing hard and complaining ill-temperedly.

"Oh! Oh!" mourned Gwendolyn. The smoke blown back from that fleeing figure smarted her throat and eyes. She raised an arm to shield her face. Disappointed, and feeling a first touch of weariness, she could not choke back a great sob that shook her convulsively.

The Man-Who-Makes-Faces, whiskers buried in his ragged collar, was nodding thoughtfully "By and by," he murmured; "—by and by, presently, later on."

The Doctor was even more comforting. "There! There!" he said. "Don't cry."

"But, oh," breathed Gwendolyn, her bosom heaving, "why don't you feel *her* pulse?"

"It's—it's terrible," faltered Gwendolyn's father. His agonized look was fixed upon the road.

Now the road was indeed terrible. For there were great chasms in it—chasms that yawned darkly; that opened and closed as if by the rush and receding of water. Gwendolyn's mother crossed them in flitting leaps, as from one roof-top to another. Her daintily shod feet scarcely touched the road, so swift was her going. A second, and she was whipped from sight at the Barn's corner. About her slender figure, as it disappeared, dust mingled with the smoke—mingled and swirled, funnel-like in shape, with a wide base and a narrow top, like the picture of a water-spout in the back of Gwendolyn's geography.

The Piper came back, wiping his forehead. "What does she care about a poke!" he scolded, flinging himself down irritably. "Huh! All she thinks about is what They say!"

At that Gwendolyn's spirits revived. Somehow, instantly and clearly, she knew what should be done!

But when she opened her mouth, she found that she could not speak. Her lips were dry. Her tongue would not move. She could only swallow.

Then, just as she was on the point of throwing herself down and giving way utterly to tears, she felt a touch on her hand—a furry touch. Next, something was slipped into her grasp. It was the lip-case!

"Well, Mr. Piper," she cried out, "what *do* They say?"

They were close by, standing side by side, gazing at nothing. For their eyes were wide open, their faces expression-less.

Gwendolyn's father addressed them. "I never asked my wife to drop that sort of thing," he said gravely, "—for Gwendolyn's sake. *You* might, I suppose." One hand was in his pocket.

The two pairs of wide-open eyes blinked once. The two mouths spoke in unison: "Money talks."

Gwendolyn's father drew his hand from his pocket. It was filled with bills. "Will these—?" he began.

It was the Piper who snatched the money out of his hand and handed it to They. And thinking it over afterward, Gwendolyn felt deep gratitude for the promptness with which They acted. For having received the money, They advanced into that terrible road, faced half-about, and halted.

The angry song of the bee was faint then. For the slender figure was speeding past those patches of light that could be seen through the girders of the Barn. But soon the buzzing grew louder—as Gwendolyn's mother came into sight, shrouded, and scarcely discernible.

They met her as she came on, blocking her way. And, "Madam!" They shouted. "Trade your bonnet for the Piper's poke!"

Gwendolyn held her breath.

Her mother halted. Now for the first time she lifted her eyes and looked about—as if dazed and miserable. There was a flush on each smooth cheek. She was panting so that her lips quivered.

The Piper rose and hurried forward. And seeing him, half-timidly she reached out a hand—a slender, white hand. Quickly he relinquished the poke, but when she took it, made a cup of his two hands under it, as if he feared she might let it fall. The poke was heavier than the bonnet. She held it low, but looked at it intently, smiling a little.

Presently, without even a parting glance, she held the bonnet out to him. "Take it away," she commanded. "It isn't becoming."

He received it; and promptly made off along the road, the bonnet held up before his face. "When it comes to chargin'," he called back, with an independent jerk of the head, "I'm the only chap that can keep ahead of a chauffeur." And he laughed uproariously.

Gwendolyn's mother now began to admire the poke, turning it around, at the same time tilting her head to one side,—this very like the Bird! She fingered the lace, and picked at the ribbon. Then, having viewed it from every angle, she opened it—as if to put it on.

There was a bounce and a piercing squeal. Then over the rim of the poke, with a thump as it hit the roadway, shot a small black-and-white pig.

She dropped the poke and sprang back, frightened. And as the porker cut away among the trees, she wheeled, caught sight of Gwendolyn, and suddenly opened her arms.

With a cry, Gwendolyn flung herself forward. No need now to fear harming an elegant dress, or roughing carefully arranged hair. "Moth-er!" She clasped her mother's neck, pressing a wet cheek against a cheek of satin.

"Oh, my baby! My baby!—Look at mother!"

"I *am* looking at you," answered Gwendolyn, half sobbing and half laughing. "I've looked at you for a *long* time. 'Cause I *love* you so I love you!"

The next moment the Man-Who-Makes-Faces dashed suddenly aside—to a nearby flower-bordered square of packed ground over which, blazing with lights, hung one huge tree. Under the tree was a high, broad bill-board, a squat stool, and two short-legged tables. The little old gentleman began to bang his furniture about excitedly.

"The tables are turned!" he shouted. "The tables are turned!"

"Of course the tables are turned," said Gwendolyn; "but what diff'rence'll *that* make?"

"Difference?" he repeated, tearing back; "it means that from now on everything's going to be exactly *opposite* to what it has been."

"Oo! Goody!" Then lifting a puzzled face. "But why didn't you turn the tables at first? And why didn't we stay here? My moth-er was here all the time. And—"

The Man-Who-Makes-Faces regarded her solemnly. "Suppose we hadn't gone around," he said. "Just suppose." Before her, in a line, were They, the Doctor, the Policeman, Puffy and the Bird. He indicated them by a nod.

She nodded too, comprehending.

"But now," went on the little old gentleman, "we must all absquatulate." He took her hand.

"Oh, must you?" she asked regretfully. Absquatulate was a big word, but she understood it, having come across it one day in the Dictionary.

"Good-by." He leaned down. And she saw that his round black eyes were clouded, while his square brush-like brows were working with the effort of keeping back his tears. "Good-by!" He stepped back out of the waiting line, turned, and made off slowly, turning the crank of the hand-organ as he went.

Now the voices of They spoke up. "We also bid you good-night," They said politely. "We shall have to go. People must hear about this." And shoulder to shoulder They wheeled and followed the little old gentleman.

"But my Puffy!" said Gwendolyn. "I'd like to keep him. I don't care if he is shabby."

For answer there was a crackling and crashing in the underbrush, as if some heavy-footed animal were lumbering away.

"I think," explained her father, "that he's gone to make some poor little boy very happy."

"Oh, the Rich Little Poor Boy, I guess," said Gwendolyn, contented.

The Bird was just in front of her. He looked very handsome and bright as he flirted his rudder saucily, and darted, now up, now down. Presently, he began to sing—a glad, clear song. And singing, rose into the air.

"Oh!" she breathed. "He's happy 'cause he got that salt off his tail." When she looked again at the line, the Policeman was nowhere to be seen. "Doctor!"

"Yes."

"Don't *you* go."

"The Doctor is right here," said her mother, soothingly.

Gwendolyn smiled. And put one hand in the clasp of her mother's, the other in a bigger grasp.

"Tired out—all tired out," murmured her father.

She was sleepy, too—almost past the keeping open of her gray eyes. "Long as you both are with me," she whispered, "I wouldn't mind if I was back in the nursery."

The glow that filled the Land now seemed suddenly to soften. The clustered tapers had lessened—to a single chandelier of four globes. Next, the forest trees began to flatten, and take on the appearance of a conventional pattern. The grass became rug-like in smoothness. The sky squared itself to the proportions of a ceiling.

There was no mistaking the change at hand!

"We're getting close!" she announced happily.

The rose-colored light was dim, peaceful. Here and there through it she caught glints of white and gold. Then familiar objects took shape. She made out the pier-glass; flanking it, her writing-desk, upon which were the two silver-framed portraits. And there—between the portraits—was the flower-embossed calendar, with pencil-marks checking off each figure in the lines that led up to her birthday.

She sighed—a deep, tremulous sigh of content.

CHAPTER XVI

She moved her head from side to side slowly. And felt the cool touch of the pillow against either cheek. Then she tried to lift her arms; but found that one hand was still in a big grasp, the other in a clasp that was softer.

Little by little, and with effort, she opened her gray eyes. In the dimness she could see, to her left, scarcely more than an outline of a dark-clad figure, stooped and watchful; of that other slender figure opposite. After all the fatigue and worry of the night, her father and mother were with her yet! And someone was standing at the foot of her bed, leaning and looking down at her. That was the Doctor.

She lay very still. This was a novel experience, this having both father and mother in the nursery at the same time—and plainly in no haste to depart! The heaviness of deep sleep was gradually leaving her. Yet she forbore to speak; and as each moment went she dreaded the passing of it, lest her wonderful new happiness come to an end.

Presently she ventured a look around—at the pink-tinted ceiling, with its cluster of full-blown plaster roses out of which branched the chandelier; at the walls of soft rose, met here and there by the deeper rose of the brocade hangings; at the plushy rug, the piano, the large table—now scattered with an unusual assortment of bottles and glasses; at the dresser, crystal-topped and strewn daintily, the deep upholstered chair, and the long cushioned seat across the front window, over which, strangely enough, no dome-topped cage was swinging.

And there was the tall toy-case. The shelves of it were unchanged. On that one below the line of prettily clad dolls were the toys she favored most— the black-and-red top, the handsome soldier in the scarlet coat, the jointed snake beside its pipe-like box, and the somersault man, poised heels over head. Beyond these, ranged in a buff row, were the six small ducks acquired at Easter. She gave each plaything a keen glance. They reminded her vividly of the long busy night just past!

Her small nose wrinkled in a quizzical smile.

At that the three waiting figures stirred.

Her look came back to them, to rest first upon her father's face, noting how long and pale and haggard it was, how sunken the temples, how bloodless the tightly pressed lips, how hollow the unshaven cheeks. When she turned to gaze at her mother, as daintily clad as ever, and as delicately perfumed—showing no evidence of dusty travel—she saw how pitifully pale was that dear beautiful face. But the eyes were no longer proud!—only anxious, tender and purple-shadowed.

Next, Gwendolyn lifted her eyes to the Doctor, and felt suddenly conscience-stricken, remembering how she had always dreaded him, had taken the mere thought of his coming as punishment; remembering, too, how helpful and kind he had been to her through the night.

He began to speak, low and earnestly, and as if continuing something already half said:

"Pardon my bluntness, but it's a bad thing when there's too much money spent on forcing the brain before the body is given a chance—or the soul. Does a child get food that is simple and nourishing, and enough of it? Is all exercise taken in the open? Too often, I find, where there's a motor at the beck and call of a nurse, the child in her charge is utterly cut off—and in the period of quickest growth—from a normal supply of plain walking. Every boy and girl has a right" (his voice deepened with feeling) "to the great world out of doors. Let the warm sun, and the fresh air, and God's good earth—"

Gwendolyn moved. "Is—is he praying?" she whispered.

There was a moment of silence. Then, "No, daughter," answered her father, while her mother leaned to lay a gentle hand on her forehead. The Doctor went aside to the larger table and busied himself with some bottles. When he came back, her father lifted her head a trifle by lifting the pillow—her mother rising quickly to assist—and the Doctor put a glass to Gwendolyn's lips. She drank dutifully, and was lowered.

At once she felt stronger. "Is the sun up?" she asked. Her voice was weak, and somewhat hoarse.

"Would you like to see the sky?" asked her father. And without waiting for her eager nod, crossed to the front window and drew aside the heavy silk hangings.

Serenely blue was the long rectangle framed by curtains and casing. Across it not a single fat sheep was straying.

"Moth-er!"

"Yes, darling?"

"Is—is always the same piece of Heaven right there through the window?"

"No. The earth is turning all the time—just as your globe in the school-room turns. And so each moment you see a new square of sky."

The Doctor nodded with satisfaction. "Um! Better, aren't we?" he inquired, smiling down.

She returned the smile. "Well, *I* am," she declared. "But—I didn't know you felt bad."

He laughed. "Tell me something," he went on. "I sent a bottle of medicine here yesterday."

"Yes. It was a little bottle."

"How much of it did Jane give you? Can you remember?"

"Well, first she poured out one teaspoonful—"

The Doctor had been leaning again on the foot of the white-and-gold bed. Now he fell back of a sudden. "A *teaspoonful!*" he gasped. And to Gwendolyn's father, "Why, that wretched girl didn't read the directions on the bottle!"

There was another silence. The two men stared at each other. But Gwendolyn's mother, her face paler than before, bent above the yellow head on the pillow.

"After I drank *that* teaspoonful," went on Gwendolyn, "Jane wouldn't believe me. And so she made me take the other."

"*Another!*"—it was the Doctor once more. He pressed a trembling hand to his forehead.

Her father rose angrily. "She shall be punished," he declared. And began to walk to and fro. "I won't let this pass."

Gwendolyn's look followed him tenderly. "Well, you see, she didn't know about—about nursery work," she explained. "'Cause before she came here she was just a cook."

"Oh, my baby daughter!" murmured Gwendolyn's mother, brokenly. She bent forward until her face was hidden against the silken cover of the bed. "Mother didn't know you were being neglected! She thought she was giving you the *best* of care, dear!"

"Two spoonfuls!" said the Doctor, grimly. "That explains everything!"

"Oh, but I didn't want to take the last one," protested Gwendolyn, hastily, "—though it tasted good. She made me. She said if I didn't—"

"So!" exclaimed the Doctor, interrupting. "She frightened the poor little helpless thing in order to get obedience!"

"Gwendolyn!" whispered her mother. "She *frightened* you?"

The gray eyes smiled wisely. "It doesn't matter now," she said, a hint of triumph in her voice. "I've found out that P'licemen are nice. And so are—are Doctors"—she dimpled and nodded. "And all the bears in the world that are outside of cages are just Puffy Bears grown up." Then uncertainly, "But I didn't find out about—the other."

"What other?" asked her father, pausing in his walk.

The gray eyes were diamond-bright now. "Though I don't *really* believe it," she hastened to add. "But—*do* wicked men keep watch of this house."

"*Wicked men?*" Her mother suddenly straightened.

"Kidnapers."

This innocent statement had an unexpected effect. Again her father began to stride up and down angrily, while her mother, head drooping once more, began to weep.

"Oh, mother didn't know!" she sobbed. "Mother didn't guess what terrible things were happening! Oh, forgive her! Forgive her!"

The Doctor came to her side. "Too much excitement for the patient," he reminded her. "Don't you think you'd better go and lie down for a while, and have a little rest?"

A startled look. And Gwendolyn put out a staying hand to her mother. Then —"Moth-er *is* tired," she assented. "She's tireder than I am. 'Cause it was hard work going round and round Robin Hood's Barn."

The Doctor hunted a small wrist and felt the pulse in it. "That's all right," he said to her mother in an undertone. "Everything's still pretty real to her, you see. But her pulse is normal," He laid cool fingers across her forehead. "Temperature's almost normal too."

Gwendolyn felt that she had not made herself altogether clear. She hastened to explain. "I mean," she said, "when moth-er was carrying that society bee in her bonnet."

Confusion showed in the Doctor's quick glance from parent to parent. Then, "I think I'll just drop down into the pantry," he said hastily, "and see how that young nurse from over yonder is getting along." He jerked a thumb in the direction of the side window as he went out.

Gwendolyn wondered just who the young nurse was. She opened her lips to ask; then saw how painfully her mother had colored at the mere mention of the person in question, and so kept silence.

The Doctor gone, her father came to her mother's side and patted a shoulder. "Well, we shan't ever say anything more about that bee," he declared, laughing, yet serious enough. "*Shall* we, Gwendolyn!"

"No." She blinked, puzzling over it a little.

"There! It's settled." He bent and kissed his wife. "You thought you were doing the best thing for our little girl—*I* know that, dear. You had her future in mind. And it's natural—and *right*—for a mother to think of making friends—the right kind, too—and a place in the social world for her daughter. And I've been short-sighted, and neglectful, and—"

"Ah!" She raised wet eyes to him. "You had your worries. You were doing *more* than your share. You had to meet the question of money. While I—"

He interrupted her. "We *both* thought we were doing our very best," he declared.

"We almost did our worst! Oh, what would it all have amounted to—what would *anything* have mattered—if we'd lost our little girl!"

The pink came rushing to Gwendolyn's cheeks. "Why, I wasn't lost at all!" she declared happily. "And, oh, it was so good to have my questions all answered, and understand so many things I didn't once—and to be where all the put-out lights go, and—and where soda-water comes from. And I was *so* glad to get rid of Thomas and Jane and Miss Royle, and—"

The hall-door opened. She checked herself to look that way. Someone was entering with a tray. It was a maid—*a maid wearing a sugar-bowl cap.*

Gwendolyn knew her instantly—that pretty face, as full and rosy as the face of the French doll, and framed by saucy wisps and curls as fair as Gwendolyn's own—and freckleless!

"Oh!" It was a low cry of delight.

The nurse smiled. She had a tray in one hand. On the tray was a blue bowl of something steaming hot. She set the tray down and came to the bed-side.

Gwendolyn's eyes were wide with wonder. "How—how—?" she began.

Her mother answered. "Jane called down to the Policeman, and he ran to the house on the corner."

Now the dimples sprang into place, "Goody!" exclaimed Gwendolyn, and gave a little chuckle.

Her mother went on: "We never can feel grateful enough to her, because she was such a help. And we're so glad you're friends already."

Gwendolyn nodded. "She's one of my window-friends," she explained.

"I'm going to stay with you," said the nurse. She smoothed Gwendolyn's hair fondly. "Will you like that?"

"It's fine! I—I wanted you!"

The Doctor re-entered. "Well, how does our sharp little patient feel now?" he inquired.

"I feel hungry."

"I have some broth for you," announced the pretty nurse, and brought forward the tray.

Gwendolyn looked down at the bowl. "M-m-m!" she breathed. "It smells good! Now"—to the Doctor—"if I had one of your nice bread-pills—"

At that, curiously enough, everyone laughed, the Doctor heartiest of all. And "Hush!" chided her mother gently while the Doctor shook a teasing finger.

"Just for that," said he, "we'll have eating—and *no* conversation—for five whole minutes." Whereupon he began to scribble on a pad, laughing to himself every now and then as he wrote.

"That must be a cheerful prescription," observed Gwendolyn's father. He himself looking happier than he had.

"The country," answered the Doctor, "is always cheerful."

Gwendolyn's spoon slipped from her fingers. She lifted eager, shining eyes. "Moth-er," she half-whispered, "does the Doctor mean *Johnnie Blake's?*"

The Doctor assented energetically. "I *prescribe* Johnnie Blake's," he declared.

"A-a-ah!" It was a deep breath of happiness. "I *promised* Johnnie that I'd come back!"

"But if my little daughter isn't strong—" Her father gave a sidewise glance at the steaming bowl on the tray.

Thus prompted, Gwendolyn fell to eating once more, turning her attention to the *croutons* bobbing about on the broth Each was square and crunchy, but not so brown as a bread-pill.

"I shall now read my Johnnie Blake prescription," announced the Doctor, and held up a leaf from the pad. "Hm! Hm!" Then, in a business-like tone; "*Take two pairs of sandals, a dozen cheap gingham dresses with plenty of pockets and extra pieces for patches, and a bottle of something good for wild black-berry scratches.*" He bowed. "*Mix all together with one strong medium-sized garden-hoe—*"

"Oh, fath-er," cried Gwendolyn, her hoarse voice wistful with pleading, "*you* won't mind if I play with Johnnie, *will* you?"

"Play all the time," answered her father. "Play hard—and then play some more."

"He *isn't* a common little boy." Whereupon, satisfied, she returned to the blue bowl.

"And now," went on the Doctor, "as to directions." He held up other leaves from the pad. "First week (you'll have to go easy the first week), use the prescription each day as follows; When driving; also when lying on back watching birds in trees (and have a nap out of doors if you feel like it); also when lighting the fire at sundown. Nurse, here, will watch out for fingers."

At that, another pleased little chuckle.

"Second week:" (the Doctor coughed, importantly) "When riding your own fat pony, or chasing butterflies—assisted by one good-natured, common, ordinary, long-haired dog; or when fishing (stream or bath-tub, it doesn't matter!) or carrying kindling in to Cook—whether you're tired or not!"

"I *love* it!"

"Third week: When baking mudpies, or gathering ferns (but put 'em in water when you get home); when jaunting in old wagon to hay-field, orchard or vegetable-patch—this includes tomboy yelling. And go barefoot."

Gwendolyn's spoon, *crouton*-laden, wabbled in mid-air. "Go *barefoot?*" she repeated, small face flushing to a pleased pink. "Right *away?* Before I'm eight?"

"Um!" assented the Doctor. "And shin up trees (but don't disturb eggs if you find 'em). Also do barefoot gardening,—where there isn't a plant to hurt! *And wade the creek.*"

Again the dimples came rushing to their places. "I like squashing," she declared, smiling round.

"Then isn't there a hill to climb?" continued the Doctor, "with your hat down your back on a string? And stones to roll—?"

The small face grew suddenly serious. "No, thank you," she said, with a slow shake of the head, "I'd rather not turn any stones."

"Very well—hm! hm!"

"Oh, and there'll be jolly times of an evening after supper," broke in her father, enthusiastically. The stern lines of his face were relaxed, and a score of tiny ripples were carrying a smile from his mouth to his tired eyes. "We'll light all the candles—"

"Daddy!" She relinquished the bowl, and turned to him swiftly. "Not—not candles that burn at both ends—"

"No." He stopped smiling.

"You're a wise little body!" pronounced the Doctor, taking her hand.

"How's the pulse now?" asked her mother. "Somehow"—with a nervous little laugh—"she makes me anxious."

"Normal," answered the Doctor promptly. "Only thing that isn't normal about her is that busy brain, which is abnormally bright." Thereupon he shook the small hand he was holding, strode to the table, and picked up a leather-covered case. It was black, and held a number of bottles. In no way did it resemble the pill-basket. "And if a certain person is to leave for the country soon—"

Gwendolyn's smile was knowing. "You mean 'a certain party.'" He was trying to tease her with that old nursery name!

"—She'd better rest. Good-by." And with that mild advice, he beckoned the nurse to follow him, whispered with her a moment at the door, and was gone.

Gwendolyn's father resumed his place beside the bed. "She *can* rest," he declared, "—the blessed baby! Not a governess or a teacher is to show as much as a hat-feather."

She nodded. "We don't want 'em quacking around."

Someone tapped at the door then, and entered—Rosa, bearing a card-tray upon which were two square bits of pasteboard. "To see Madam," she said, presenting the tray. After which she showed her white teeth in greeting to Gwendolyn, then stooped, and touched an open palm with her lips.

Gwendolyn's mother read the cards, and shook her head. "Tell the ladies— explain that I can't leave my little daughter even for a moment to-day—"

"Oh, yes, Madam."

"And that we're leaving for the country *very* soon."

Rosa bobbed her dark head as she backed away.

"And, Rosa—"

"Yes, Madam?"

"You know what I need in the country—where we were before."

A bow.

"Pack, Rosa. And you will go, of course."

"And Potter, Madam?"

"Potter, too. You'll have to pack a few things up here also." A white hand indicated the wardrobe door.

"Very well, Madam."

As the door closed, the telephone rang. Gwendolyn's father rose to answer it. "I think it's the office, dear," he explained; and into the transmitter —"Yes?... Hello?... Yes. Good-morning!... Oh, thanks! She's better.... And by the way, just close out that line of stocks. Yes.... I shan't be back in the office for some time. I'm leaving for the country as soon as Gwendolyn can stand the trip. To-morrow, maybe, or the next day.... No; don't go into the market until I come back. I intend to reconstruct my policy a good deal. Yes.... Oh, yes.... Good-by."

He went to the front window. And as he stood in the light, Gwendolyn lay and looked at him. He had worn green the night before. But now there was not a vestige of paper money showing anywhere in his dress. In fact, he was wearing the suit—a dark blue—he had worn that night she penetrated to the library.

"Fath-er."

"Well, little daughter?"

"I was wondering has anybody scribbled on the General's horse?—with chalk?"

Her father looked down at the Drive. "The General's there!" he announced, glancing back at her over a shoulder. "And his horse seems in *fine* fettle this morning, prancing, and arching his neck. And nobody's scribbled on him, which seems to please the General very much, for he's got his hat off—"

Gwendolyn sat up, her eyes rounding. "To hundreds and hundreds of soldiers!" she told her mother. "Only everybody can't see the soldiers."

Her father came back to her. "*I* can," he declared proudly. "Do you want to see 'em, too?—just a glimpse, mother! Come! We'll play the game together!" And the next moment, silk coverlet and all, Gwendolyn was swung up in his arms and borne to the window-seat.

"And, oh, there's the P'liceman!" she cried out.

"His name is Flynn," informed her father. "And *twice* this morning he's asked after you."

"Oh!" she stood up among the cushions to get a better view. "He takes lost little boys and girls to their fath-ers and moth-ers, daddy, and he takes care of the trees, and the flowers, and the fountains, and—- and the ob'lisk. But he only likes it up here in summer. In winter he likes to be Down-Town. And he *ought* to be Down-Town, 'cause he's got a *really* level head—"

"Wave to him now," said her father. "There! He's swinging his cap!—When we're out walking one of these times we'll stop and shake hands with him!"

"With the hand-organ man, too, fath-er? Oh, you like him, *don't* you? And you won't send him away!"

"Father won't."

He laid her back among the pillows then. And she turned her face to her mother.

"Can't you sleep, darling?—And don't dream!"

"Well, I'm pretty tired."

"We know what a hard long night it was."

"Oh, I'm *so* glad we're going back to Johnnie Blake's, moth-er. 'Cause, oh, I'm tired of pretending!"

"Of pretending," said her father. "Ah, yes."

Her mother nodded at him. "I'm tired of pretending, too," she said in a low voice.

Gwendolyn looked pleased. "I didn't know you ever pretended," she said. "Well, of course, you know that *real* things are so much nicer—"

"Ah, yes, my little girl!" It was her father. His voice trembled.

"Real grass,"—she smiled up at him—"and real trees, and real people." After that, for a while, she gave herself over to thinking. How wonderful that one single night could bring about the changes for which she had so longed!—the living in the country; the eating at the grown-up table, and having no governess.

One full busy night had done all that! And yet—

She glanced down at herself. Under her pink chin was the lace and ribbon of a night-dress. She could not remember being put to bed—could not even recall coming up in the bronze cage. And was the plaid gingham with the patch-pocket now hanging in the wardrobe? Brows knit, she slipped one small foot sidewise until it was close to the edge of the bed-covers, then of a sudden thrust it out from beneath them. The foot was as white as if it had only just been bathed! Not a sign did it show of having waded any stream, pattered through mud, or trudged a forest road!

Presently, "Moth-er,"—sleepily.

"Yes, darling?"

"*Who* are Law and Order?"

A moment's silence. Then, "Well—er—"

"Isn't it a fath-er-and-moth-er question?"

"Why, *yes*, my baby. But I—"

"Father will tell you, dear." He was seated beside her once more. "You see it's this way:"

"Can you tell it like a story, fath-er?"

"Yes."

"A once-upon-a-time story?"

"I'll try. But first you must understand that law and order are not two people. Oh, no. And they aren't anything a little girl could see—as she can see the mirror, for instance, or a chair—"

Gwendolyn looked at the mirror and the chair—thence around the room. These were the same things that had been there all the time. Now how different each appeared! There was the bed, for instance. She had never liked the bed, beautiful though it was. Yet to-day, even with the sun shining on the great panes of the wide front window, it seemed good to be lying in it. And the nursery, once a hated place—a very prison!—the nursery had never looked lovelier!

Her father went on with his explaining, low and cheerily, and as confidentially as if to a grown-up. Across from him, listening, was her mother, one soft cheek lowered to rest close to the small face half-hidden in the pillow.

When her father finished speaking, Gwendolyn gave a deep breath—of happiness and content. Then, "Moth-er!"

"Yes?"—with a kiss as light as the touch of a butterfly.

Her eyelids, all at once, seemed curiously heavy. She let them flutter down. But a drowsy smile curved the pink mouth. "Moth-er," she whispered; "moth-er, the Dearest Pretend has come true!"

www.ingramcontent.com/pod-product-compliance
Lightning Source LLC
Chambersburg PA
CBHW080908190726
48294CB00008B/2005